A LITTLE NIGHT MURDER

MYDWORTH MYSTERIES #2

Neil Richards • Matthew Costello

RED DOG
UK

A LITTLE NIGHT MURDER

PROLOGUE

Syd Buckman stepped carefully over the rickety fence onto the old Arundel road, put down his canvas bag, and stood to listen.

Slowly, his ears tuned to the sounds of the night.

Up on the far hill, in the dark woods, he heard an owl hooting. He waited for an answering call. Sure enough, *there it was,* maybe half a mile away.

From down in the valley, he could just hear distant voices. He couldn't see Mydworth from here, but he knew that sound well: *chucking out time at the King's Arms.* He fancied he even recognised the laughter, and smiled to himself.

The usual lot, reluctant to wobble home to the not-so-patient wife!

A faint rustling sound from the field ahead made him quickly turn. In the dim light from the thin sliver of moon above, he could see the lines of tall wheat disappearing into the darkness.

Fox maybe? No. Something smaller.

Satisfied he was on his own up here, he picked up the bag, hoisted it over his shoulder, and set off up the road towards the far hill and woods.

Past eleven now, and he didn't expect to meet anyone. Pubs all closed. And the good – and not so good – people of Sussex would soon be in their beds, sleeping the sleep of the righteous or the addled.

The good people of Sussex, he thought. *Doesn't include me, that's for sure.*

He smiled to himself, and switched the bag to his other shoulder.

Wasn't heavy. But awkward.

Not easy to hide a Lee Enfield rifle.

His dad's old canvas army bag wasn't long enough to conceal the barrel, and the grey steel of the muzzle peeped out through the rope ties at one end.

But on a dark night like this, Syd knew that if he held the bag tight to his side, the casual observer wouldn't notice the business end of the lethal firearm poking out.

Don't want to frighten some old fella walking home after a few pints.

Or worse – some nosy copper looking for trouble.

Not tonight.

He had work to do.

TEN MINUTES later, Syd reached the familiar curve in the road where the Shreeve Estate began. Here the fence met a sturdy brick wall that he knew ran for miles: tracking the line of the road for a mile, before turning north to encircle the main house, then returning to where he stood.

Enclosing a thousand acres of woodland, meadows, hills and valleys. Herds of cattle. Flocks of sheep.

And deer.

Hundreds of deer, roaming free.

Each one worth a pretty penny *if* you knew the right butcher.

And Syd Buckman knew the right butcher.

All he had to do was deliver the goods.

No question – he knew how to do that. Like his dad – and his dad's dad before him.

Reckon us Buckmans been working these woods all the way back to that bastard William the Conqueror. Wasn't he the one took 'em off the people, made them royal hunting grounds?

Syd spat onto the dusty road. Then he walked along the wall until he spied the loose bricks he'd chiselled away a month or so back – perfect footholds if you knew where they were.

He pulled himself up easily and, in an instant, he was over the wall and crouching on the other side in the musty darkness of the woods.

He pulled the bag from his shoulder and took out the rifle, pointing it carefully at the ground.

"Don't matter how sure you are it's not loaded – always treat a gun like it is," his dad had taught him when he was a nipper.

And though the old bugger was a drunken, nasty piece of work, he knew what he was talking about when it came to guns.

Syd felt the weight of the weapon. He loved the familiar oiled metal and wood smell – the smooth, worn feel of the stock.

He reached into his pocket and took out the cartridges – brass cases, long, pointed.

With a crack shot – lethal.

He flicked the safety off, pulled back the bolt and – one by one – slotted five rounds into the magazine.

Gently, he slid the bolt home – the action so smooth and quiet – and put the safety catch back on.

Slinging the bag over his shoulder again, he stood, and with the gun held securely in both hands, he walked slowly into the deep, dark wood, his boots making no sound on the soft, mossy ground.

His whole body, all his senses, alive to the smells, the sounds, the very feel of the living forest.

His eyes alert for any tell-tale signs of deer – tracks, droppings. Tree bark marked by the bucks rubbing their antlers.

This moment – always so exciting. Feeling so alive.

Even with the danger of being caught.

No turning back now: loaded gun in hand, there could be no denying what he was doing out here in the middle of the night on a private estate. And only one word for it—*Poaching.*

SYD SAT, with his back against an ancient oak tree, the rifle resting on his lap, his breathing light, his whole body alert to the movements of the forest.

He'd come across the herd of deer an hour ago and had walked, crouching, a half mile round them to end up here concealed in the darkness of the woods, downwind of his prey on the edge of a grassy clearing.

Ready for them.

He knew they would come this way, following the line of clearings, stopping, feeding a while, browsing in shrubs and then moving on.

Unaware they were getting closer and closer to their hunter.

And now they were here.

He could just see the stag through the trees – head still, antlers tall – the great beast pausing at the front of the herd before leading them slowly in this direction.

Behind him, Syd saw the other deer, heads down again, grazing. Now and then looking up nervously as they heard a sound; stopping as one, and staring intently into the woods, before returning to their steady munching of grass.

They hadn't seen him, and, as long as he didn't move a muscle, they wouldn't.

He scanned the herd, now just fifty yards away, selecting his target.

There. That one at the back: a young buck, fine-looking animal; fit and healthy; not too heavy to carry.

He'd seen the same buck the last two or three times he'd been up here in the woods, and marked it down as a possible target.

Much as he'd love to take down the big stag, Syd knew he'd need a gang with him to carry *that* carcass out of the woods. But the buck? Oh yes, he could manage that on his own.

As if the creature had heard him, it looked up, staring in Syd's direction, eyes soft, dark – almost trusting.

Always such a great moment.

Syd held his breath – and the buck finally looked away, then moved into the centre of the clearing, away from the other deer, and started feeding again.

Perfect.

Slowly he eased the safety catch to "off", raised the rifle, nestling the heavy stock into his shoulder, and drew the gun to his face.

He pressed his cheek against the warm wood, again smelling the gun-oil, eyes focusing on the iron sights, the buck's head perfectly lined up in the "v".

He saw the deer look up again from the grass, as if sensing the deadly moment to come. Syd followed the movement of the head with his rifle, breathed out gently, squeezed the trigger… and slowly *pulled.*

Bang! The sound of the shot crashed through the woods, unbelievably loud. He saw the young buck drop stone dead in the clearing – and the other deer fleeing, leaping, madly flying through the trees to escape.

Syd lowered the rifle and clicked the safety back on.

Important not to rush that!

Then he picked up the ejected cartridge case, slid it into his pocket and got to his feet, his back and legs aching from the long wait.

He walked over to the deer, which lay motionless in the clearing. He could see where the round had taken the animal cleanly in the head. *Stone-cold dead. Such a clean shot.*

He put his bag down on the ground and took out ropes and a knife. This was the hard part – strapping the carcass up so he could carry it the long mile hike back to the road.

That shot would have been heard miles away – and though a single shot would be impossible to locate in an estate this size, he knew he had to move smartish.

Get caught like this – red-handed – it would be a prison sentence for sure.

Not a risk Syd wanted to take.

HE'D GONE half a mile when he heard a sound in the woods behind him. Only a twig breaking. But Syd knew it takes weight to break a twig on a forest floor, and he also knew there were only a few creatures heavy enough to do that.

A deer. A wild boar, maybe.

Or a human.

He stopped and turned slowly, staring into the dark trees, looking for movement.

The carcass of the deer felt heavy on his back. He had to get going. Whatever it was he'd heard, it had to be some distance away.

Or maybe I imagined it, he thought.

But, five minutes later, another sound behind him. A branch moving, snapping. Closer this time. Again, he stopped, peered into the darkness.

Pulse beginning to race.

Syd didn't like *this*.

He stepped off the path, crouched low, moved as silently as he could into the thick brush and shrubs.

Then turned and peered back along the track.

But the night had clouded over, and now there wasn't even that slither of moon to help him see.

He felt that first shiver of fear.

Something's following me. Something − or somebody…

Following.

No, not following.

Tracking.

He licked his lips, his mouth dry. Had to get out of here, fast − no question. But the deer − so heavy − was slowing him down.

Should he just dump it here? Cover it with leaves, branches?

But he was *so* close to the road − couldn't be more than five minutes now.

And he needed this money − needed it badly.

He waited, the woods silent again. Only the pounding of his heart, his own breathing, audible.

Come on Syd, he told himself, *stop monkeying around. Nobody out here, damn it! Never is.*

He hoisted the buck higher on his shoulders and turned, ready to make one last dash to the edge of the woods.

But as he turned, he saw a shape moving fast towards him.

Fast, like some kind of… *ghost*. A terrible creature of the night. And before he could even drop the buck to the ground to free his arms, to defend himself…

A LITTLE NIGHT MURDER

The creature was just a yard away. Not a creature – but a man, holding high a piece of wood. Or was that a length of iron – in his hands? The heavy object swinging already through the air, coming at his head, no time to get his own hands in the way before—

Smash – into his face, suddenly tasting blood in his mouth – teeth splintering, his head jerking backwards and then—Darkness.

And nothing more.

1.

DOMESTIC BLISS

Kat Reilly stood at the window of the Dower House guest bedroom and looked down at her husband as he worked outside on his old motorbike in the lazy Saturday morning sunshine.

Overalls on and sleeves rolled up − not the Harry she knew!

Yet he looked *completely* at home, crouched amongst the oily engine parts. As she watched him whistling to himself, wiping a greasy hand on his forehead to brush a lock of dark hair away, she felt − in quite a different way − a surge of affection for the Brit she'd married.

"See, Kat − it's all about the simple things," he'd said to her back in Cairo, as he explained why he didn't want to them to move into Mydworth Manor, the domain of his aunt, Lady Lavinia − preferring instead the much humbler house on the edge of the town.

Humble? she thought. *Well that's kinda relative − four bedrooms and an acre of garden isn't "humble" back where I come from in the Bronx, New York City.*

Where an 8-foot by 8-foot front plot of ivy passed as a "garden" for most people...

But now, having lived here in this house and this small Sussex town for a few weeks, Kat felt she understood better exactly what he'd meant.

And also just what kind of man she'd really married.

Sure, Harry liked the big city, the excitement, the influential job in the diplomatic world.

But now she knew he also liked the quiet times, the *small* things: Sunday afternoons in the garden, falling asleep over the newspapers; country walks; boat trips down the river; those funny local cricket matches and the cream teas after; evenings in the garden of the White Rose, down on the river, drinking ale.

And – surprise, surprise – she liked them too. Even liked doing up this old house, ordering new curtains, wallpaper, carpets.

Oh, and helping Maggie the housekeeper with the menus and the cooking (when she was allowed – bit of a protocol in place for all that).

Shopping in Mydworth, always fun when people looked up at her when she spoke the King's English by way of the Bronx, New York! And she was even enjoying learning how these English towns worked, who was who, what not to say and when not to say it.

A lot of unspoken rules here, she knew.

But in the back of her mind an uncomfortable thought had also begun to fight for space in the last couple of weeks.

A question to which she didn't know the answer.

Is this it? *Is this all my life is going to be?*

Forever?

Sure, children down the road. When they were ready, but…

Bubbling underneath was another unbidden question that clamoured for an answer:

How is it that I can I love Harry so much… and yet worry that maybe I'm not going to be completely happy with this?

Not… satisfied?

As if he could read her thoughts (*and she sometimes felt he really could*), she saw Harry look up at the window and give her a wave, his amazing smile so open and honest and true it made her feel guilty for having such thoughts.

She waved back, and slid open the window.

"How's it going, Mr Mechanic?" she said.

"Nearly finished. Have the old girl up and running in no time at all."

She looked at the scattered parts: "Really? 'She' looks like… well… still all in pieces."

"Oh, that? Not to worry – the hard part's done," he said grinning. "Just got to stick all the bits together – then Bob's your uncle!"

And there was another thing. These little – *dunno* – odd phrases people used over here.

Kat had learned to simply let them "pop" up. In most cases, easy enough to figure out the meaning.

In most cases.

"Hmm, I keep hearing about this Bob guy – you're going to have to introduce me one day. Fancy a tea?"

"Love one. Kitchen in a minute?"

"It's a date," she said, pulling the window closed and heading downstairs.

HARRY SCRUBBED his hands in the big scullery sink, rubbing the powdered floor cleaner on his palms to get rid of the engine grease. Ordinary soap never worked. Floor cleaner? Perfect!

The old bike – a powerful BSA – had been his pride and joy when he came back from the Front in '18, and he'd spent a joyous summer roaring through the lanes of Sussex and Kent on it, before his first diplomatic posting abroad came through.

Since then the machine had stood unused, but not forgotten, in his Aunt Lavinia's stables, covered in a tarpaulin. Now that he was back home, he was determined to get it up and running again.

And not only that… teach Kat how to ride it. His guess? She'd be a natural.

Much as he loved the Alvis (great fun for day-to-day runs round the countryside) he had to admit that on the bike – boy! – they could have some real fun together.

Another few hours' work, and the machine would be all set to go.

He dried his hands and went through into the kitchen, where he saw Kat and Maggie the housekeeper standing by the new refrigerator, door wide open.

Thing even had an ice-box. Country life was certainly changing!

"How we getting on with the tea and biscuits?" he said. "The workers need sustenance!"

"Biscuits we can do," said Kat, over her shoulder, "but…"

"The tea might take a little longer, sir," said Maggie, holding a jug of milk in her hands. Or rather – frozen milk.

"I can't do with this machine, sir," she said, turning the jug upside down to show the ice.

"Teething troubles?" said Harry, going over to join them, and inspecting the inside of the device.

"Break your teeth on this milk more like," said Maggie, slamming the jug down on the table.

"I'll take a look at that – what's it called? – thermostat, soon as I'm done with the bike," said Harry.

"I can't for the *life* of me see why we can't just use the pantry like we always did," said Maggie going over to the stove and

12

pouring boiling water from the kettle into the teapot. "These new-fangled gadgets... more trouble than they're worth, if you ask me!"

"Price of progress," Harry said. "It's the modern age, Maggie. We must all surrender to it."

Harry winked at Kat, but – strange – he noticed Kat didn't wink back.

"I just don't like it, sir," said Maggie, stirring the teapot. "All this progress! New-fangled this, new-fangled that! Where's it all going to end?"

Then Kat reached out. Gave Maggie's hand a quick, light squeeze.

Is she something or what? Harry thought.

"I'm sure you'll get used to it," said Kat. "Back in New York, well, everything's electric now you know. Carpet cleaners. Washing machines. Cars everywhere. Horse and buggies... well... soon they'll all be gone!"

Harry started on the biscuits.

"Well, I don't know," said Maggie. "I grew up on elbow grease and carbolic, like my mum and her mum before her. Us women of England – I reckons we actually *like* doing things the difficult way!"

Kat laughed at that. "Think on this, Maggie. The days of women slaving over a sink are soon coming to an end," said Kat. "Don't you think—"

"Oh, hang on there. I think I'll be out of a job if we're not all careful," said Maggie, finally bringing the teapot and cups to the table. "And I know a lot of women as thinks exactly the same—"

"Delicious biscuits," said Harry, lifting up the plate. "How about we call a truce on progress, and give thanks to whoever invented ginger nuts?"

He saw both women stare at him, arms folded – his attempt at resolving the question clearly not working for either of them.

A LITTLE NIGHT MURDER

He shrugged and gave them both his biggest grin – his weapon of last resort in such situations – though he knew, at this moment, it was probably not going to be effective.

But then he heard the telephone ring – its loud jarring sound making Maggie jump.

The old dear not used to that *either!*

"Saved by the bell, I do believe," he said, chipping at the frozen milk with his teaspoon.

"I'll answer it," said Kat, and he watched her walk out of the kitchen and down the hall.

"Shall I be mother?" he said to Maggie, lifting the pot and pouring the teas.

And at last, Maggie, wrestling with all things new here, smiled.

KAT UNHOOKED the earpiece and put it to her ear.

"Mydworth 429," said Kat.

"Lady Mortimer please," came a woman's voice.

"Speaking," said Kat, though she still hadn't got used to answering to that title.

"Ah. Right. Nicola Green here."

Kat waited, not recognising the name.

"From the WVS," continued the woman.

"I'm sorry, but…?"

"Oh of course. I'd forgotten. You're *American*. The Women's Voluntary Service."

"Ah, I see," said Kat, not seeing at all.

"We're a charity. Fighting the good fight for the women of England."

"Sounds like a good cause, indeed. You're… wanting contributions?"

"Dear me, no! The vicar said I should contact you. Said you might be able to help me."

"The vicar?"

"You did some… *work*… for him last month. Very effective, he said. And very discrete."

Now Kat began to understand. Barely a week after she and Harry had arrived from Cairo, they had helped the Reverend Elliot track down a large silver plate that had gone missing from Mydworth Church.

The vicar had been keen not to involve the police – and he'd persuaded Kat and Harry that they were just the people to investigate the theft.

As it happened – they were, and the silver was returned. An accident, the church warden had claimed. Somehow the valuable plate had ended up being taken home.

With the desperate culprit admonished – and forgiven – the whole story had been quietly forgotten.

Kept under wraps supposedly – at least that was the deal.

The vicar had even, amazingly, offered to help the thief and his family, in such dire straits. "I assume Reverend Elliot didn't pass on details," said Kat.

"Good Lord, *no*," said Nicola. "But, he did say you and Sir Harry were the closest thing Mydworth had to," and here the woman chuckled at the phrase, "a private detective agency."

Kat couldn't quite believe what she'd heard. "Really? Well…" And Kat laughed as well.

Detectives? Hardly.

"We just, well… helped him. That's all."

"I understand. *Completely*. The local police, um, are excellent at enforcing the country's licensing laws, Lady Mortimer," said

Nicola. "But their powers of detection leave a lot to be desired. Which is why I'm calling you and Sir Harry now."

"Mrs Green—"

"*Miss* Green, please."

"My apologies. Miss Green, my husband and I just helped the vicar out of a sense of community spirit. Wasn't really anything…"

"Of *course*. In the same way you apprehended those thieves at Mydworth Manor? The whole town knows about that! And very plucky you were, if my sources are correct in what they tell me!"

Kat had the feeling that her ability to decline whatever Miss Green was calling about was winnowing away by the moment.

"That was something quite different. A family matter. Unfortunate business, and we were just—"

"Yes, and a family matter is *exactly* why I'm telephoning you now. A local family, a well-meaning Mydworth family, may have suffered a great injustice. And I believe, if I'm correct, you two might help right that injustice."

"Miss Green—"

"Nicola, please."

What? thought Kat. *Now we're on first-name terms and we haven't even met. How did that happen?*

Doesn't seem very British!

"We really have no intention of playing 'detective'. The very thought – I don't know, Nicola – sounds crazy, hmm? My husband often works in London. And I have a very busy schedule here."

"I know, I *know*. Which is why today's perfect – being a Saturday. How about two o'clock in my office? You can't miss it – on Market Square above the dress shop. You know it?"

"Well, yes, I do—"

There were corners of Mydworth yet to be explored. But the square? Already Kat felt at home there.

16

"Good. Two it is then."

Silence. Kat shook her head, baffled by the course the conversation had so quickly taken.

But at the same time, *she was intrigued.* And, she had to admit– *Excited.*

She took a deep breath.

"Okay, Nicola, I will come at two. *Possibly* – and only 'possibly' – with my husband. That is entirely up to him. And not as a detective. But perhaps just to lend you support if you feel an injustice has been done."

"Excellent!"

"However—"

"Yes?"

"You must tell me what this is all about. Now. Briefly. On the telephone."

"About? Oh, that's very easy, Lady Mortimer. It's about a murder."

"What?"

"Yes, a murder. Right here, in Mydworth. And the culprit is *still* out there – who knows – ready to kill again."

"God…"

Call that unexpected, Kat thought.

"Exactly," said Nicola. "So. There we are. See you at two."

And Kat heard the click as the connection went dead.

A murder, thought Kat.

Well whaddya know?

2.

THE CASE BEGINS

Harry walked with Kat down the narrow cobbled lane that led into Mydworth's Market Square, the shade from the tight cluster of buildings providing a welcome relief from the suddenly hot mid-day sun.

Harry could see that the Saturday market stalls were already being wrapped up. But there were still plenty of people in the street, and he nodded to familiar faces as they passed – tipping his hat to some.

"Is there anyone at all in this town you don't know?" said Kat.

"Only the wrong kind of people. Tend to avoid them, y'know."

"Really? You actually have the 'wrong kind of people' here? In this gorgeous story-book place? Sounds fun. I *must* meet them."

"Oh, I'm sure the way you carry on – *detective* – you'll find them without my help," said Harry, laughing.

"You can take the girl outta the Bronx, hmm?"

"You said it," said Harry as they reached the square. "One of these days, we'll take a Cunard liner to New York, to see this fabled Bronx of yours!"

Kat laughed at that. "Oh! That would be something indeed, Sir Harry."

He looked around. "Dress shop. I have to say, that's one place I really don't remember."

"Doubt you'd have much call to visit. Ah – there it is," said Kat, pointing to a tiny shop that faced the market.

Harry looked over, and yes, there, in the window, stood a pair of mannequins apparently displaying the latest fashions to hit Mydworth – all bows and frills and funny little hats that looked, to Harry, like acorns.

Fashion. Now that was a world he did not understand at all.

"Yes. Can't say I've ever been in here," he said, as they approached the shop together and paused outside. "Do you think I'm even allowed?"

"Best behaviour and I'll vouch for you," said Kat, pushing open the door and making a bell ring inside.

Harry followed her in and shut the door behind him.

INSIDE HE SAW rails of clothes, hats on shelves, rolls of material, more mannequins standing tightly in the back, modelling everything from tennis skirts to cocktail gowns, looking as if attending a rather odd party.

"Can I help you?" said a woman from behind the counter in a vivid pink dress and bright make-up.

Harry watched the woman hurry round and approach them, smile too bright, teeth sparkling: "How lovely that you're choosing madame's outfit *together*! Our summer line is *so* popular at the moment."

Quickly into sales mode.

"Actually, we're looking for the WVS?" said Kat.

"Oh, I *see*," said the woman, her smile fading, a sale vanishing. "Miss Green? *Think* she's in. Up the stairs there, door on the right, just knock."

Harry nodded to the woman who returned to her counter without looking back at them, and then followed Kat up the narrow staircase.

These last few weeks with Kat have opened up a whole new side to Mydworth that I never knew existed, he thought.

A dress shop! First time for everything.

KAT KNOCKED on a door marked WVS and waited.

"It's open – come on in," came a cheery female voice from within.

She stepped through, Harry behind her, into a tiny, cramped office. All she could see at first were stacked boxes and files, the room absolutely floor-to-ceiling with books and paperwork, heavy metal cabinets – and, at the far end, a desk, some chairs, and a woman balanced on a high rung of a perilously shaky ladder.

"Grab these, would you?" said the woman, reaching down with a handful of dusty files. Kat saw Harry rush to grasp them before the whole lot scattered, and put them on the desk.

"Moving in?" said Harry.

"Unfortunately – no! Being kicked out," said the woman, coming down the ladder two steps at a time. "Her, downstairs… wants us out."

"Wrong kind of people?" said Kat, winking at Harry.

"Ha, exactly," said the woman, putting out her hand to shake theirs. "Nicola Green," she said.

"Kat," said Kat. "And my husband, Harry."

"Kat and Harry."

Nicola seemed comfortable dispensing with the formal titles. *Good,* Kat thought.

"Wonderful. Get confused by all this 'Lord and Lady' nonsense. Oh. Sorry, I don't mean to—"

"Not to worry. I'm a Yank. Talk about confused..." said Kat, smiling.

"Me too," said Harry, smiling.

Kat watched Nicola stand back – as if appraising them.

She was younger than Kat had expected – in fact, like her, probably no more than thirty. Tall, strong-featured, short, dark hair with what looked like a natural curl. Slacks, silk blouse – and a man's waistcoat.

Could be a poet, thought Kat. *Or an artist. Just needs a smock and a beret to finish off the look.*

Above all – the look of a modern woman.

"You clear those chairs while I put the kettle on," she said, pointing to two office chairs with books piled high, then heading over to a tiny sink and kitchen area. "Oh, and don't worry about Monty, he won't bite."

Kat looked for Monty and, on cue, an elderly Labrador rose sluggishly from under the desk and came over to greet them.

"Don't be fooled by that show of affection," said Nicola, returning and dumping a plate of biscuits on the desk. "He just knows when these are coming out."

She slid the plate towards them: "Tuck in. We've got a lot to talk about."

"Murder," said Kat, reaching for a biscuit.

"Murder indeed," said Nicola, already eating one.

"I'll start at the beginning," said Nicola, when all three were settled at the desk with their teas.

Harry felt Monty nuzzling persistently at his hand, and he let the dog rest his head on his lap, while Kat sneaked him a morsel of biscuit.

Harry made a mental note. *We need to get a dog!*

"The man: Syd Buckman, twenty years old, occasional farm labourer, general 'lad about town' as they say, and, pretty well-known as an inveterate poacher." Another bite of a biscuit. "Found dead two weeks ago, up on the Shreeve Estate."

"Ah yes," said Harry. "I think I read about that in the *Mydworth Mercury*. An accident, the article said."

"You probably did read that – though they didn't give much away. The lad was discovered by the estate manager, Fred Nailor, at around ten o'clock on the morning of the 15th: a bullet right through his chest and the carcass of a young deer by his side."

"Ah. An unfortunate poaching accident?" said Harry. "Open and shut case?"

"Well, the police assumed so, and so the coroner certified. The lad – it was said – appeared to have slipped on his way home with his ill-gotten spoils. Gun went off – *bang-bang*, you're dead."

"But you, um, don't agree with that account?" said Kat.

"His mother certainly doesn't," said Nicola. "Which is why I'm involved. Poor thing came here yesterday, still sobbing, begging me to do *something*! Find someone to help. Insisted that what was said to have happened could not have. And after listening to her, I'm inclined to think she may be right."

"Reasons?" said Harry.

"First, she says Syd, well, he was no angel. But he was a clever lad. And he was safe as houses around guns."

"Easy enough to fall foul of a hunting rifle," said Harry, not convinced by any of this. "Could happen to anyone."

"*Not* her Syd, his mum said," said Nicola. "Apparently his dad – who also had a penchant for a little… *night-time recreation*… beat gun safety into him as a boy. Something to do with an uncle who *wasn't* so careful."

"So young Syd knew what he was doing with a firearm?" said Kat. "That wouldn't be enough to change a coroner's report."

"No," said Nicola. "But, you see, that's not all. Apparently, there'd been some… incidents… in recent weeks. Arguments. Fights. Threats."

"What kind of threats?" said Harry.

"Death threats."

"Ah," said Harry. "Very nasty."

He looked at Kat, who gave him the slightest of nods.

Death threats. Maybe this was worth digging into.

KAT TOOK a small notebook out of her pocket, and a pencil.

"Let me get a few details if I may…" she said. "Names, you know the sort of thing."

She saw Nicola smile at the appearance of the notebook.

As if confirming her designation of the two of them as detectives!

Ridiculous…

"Let's start with Syd's mother, Elsie," said Nicola. "Still lives with his father Billy – God knows how or why, I've been telling her for years to kick the old drunk out."

"Sorry – is that the sort of thing you do here, at the WVS?" said Harry.

"Meddle, you mean?" said Nicola, turning to him.

Kat could see Nicola's eyes narrow.

"Not at all," said Harry, smiling. *Disarming.* "Sorry – I didn't put that at all right. Apologise if I sounded rude," he continued. "What I mean is – do you *advise* the good women of Mydworth, even on matters such as this?"

"Well, yes," said Nicola. "That is exactly what we do. Advise. Help. Support. No matter the situation. Women may have got the vote – at last! – but they still get a damned rough deal in this world. And that just isn't fair, is it?"

"Absolutely," said Kat. "Things changing. Just not fast enough, in my opinion."

"Whether it's a pregnant daughter, or a husband who's beating a wife, or a problem at work – I *always* have an open door. And if I don't know the answer, the WVS has supporters who do."

"Free service?" said Harry.

"*Totally.*"

"How do you survive?" said Kat.

"We barely do. In fact – as of this coming Saturday – we don't have an office."

"That's terrible," said Kat.

"It's not the first time, and it won't be the last," said Nicola. "But that's beside the point. I'll manage. The WVS will manage. But it's Syd Buckman's possible murder we're talking about. And his poor mother who's out of her wits with doubts. Can you imagine? They live in a little cottage out on Briar Lane, by the way. Off Station Road. Might I suggest you start with them?"

"Start?" said Kat.

"Elsie will tell you more about what her Syd was up against in the town. Or rather – *who* he was up against. And Billy can tell you about guns – if he's sober enough."

Kat watched Nicola look away as if what she said next might be... *a tad controversial.*

"I, er, wouldn't bother with Sergeant Timms. I tried but he told me where to go. Politely, of course. Though – on second thoughts – he *might* speak to you *Sir Harry.*"

Kat saw her smile at Harry, the nudge clear enough.

"Oh, in that case, I shall order him to," said Harry. "Isn't it in the rule book somewhere that all citizens have to do precisely what we say?"

Kat looked at Harry.

He's on board, she thought. *Good. Because I'm already there.*

"Any other suggestions?" Kat said.

"Definitely worth talking to Fred Nailor, the chap who found the body," said Nicola. "Nice man, quiet – lives up on the Shreeve Estate."

"Ah," said Harry. "So, Syd was poaching Shreeve's deer, was he?"

"You know Mr Shreeve?" said Nicola.

"Who doesn't?" said Harry. "Kind of a big deal, even before I went out East."

Kat expected him to say more, but he didn't. From the look she saw pass between Harry and Nicola she guessed Mr Shreeve had a bit of a story – a story she needed to hear.

"So – anything else you need from me?" said Nicola. "Only I really must finish this packing."

Kat turned to Harry and gave him a quick smile, as they both got up from the table.

Seems we got the job – and we didn't even know we were applying for it. Job? Or is it... a case?

"One last thing," she said, turning back to Nicola. "If we go around town asking questions, it's going to be pretty obvious we're doing this for you. Is that okay?"

"Oh – I'm not worried about that. Mydworth already regards me as the official troublemaker, you see. You couldn't possibly make my reputation any worse. Least with a lot of the menfolk!"

"Hmm – I wouldn't be too sure about that," said Harry. "If you knew Kat, like I know Kat…"

Nicola laughed. "Just don't go hitting people on my behalf, Kat. Although on second thoughts – let me dig out that list of candidates for a right hook."

Kat laughed. Earlier in the summer she'd had to take down a fleeing suspect and news of the event had travelled widely. "That little incident a few weeks back? Well, that was just a lucky punch."

"I always say, you make your own luck in a fight," said Nicola.

And I bet you've been in a few yourself, thought Kat, instantly liking this woman.

"How shall we find you if we need more information?" said Harry.

"Just leave a note behind the bar at the King's Arms," said Nicola. "Old Johnny Fox will hold it for me. Seems the owner at the Arms believes in what I'm doing here. And I'll telephone you. Good luck."

Kat watched her turn back to her packing.

Has to be tough moving all this.

"We'll do our best," said Kat. "Sure we can't give you a hand here?"

"Very kind of you. But please, don't you worry. I've got an army of helpers coming tomorrow to do the heavy lifting. The good ladies of Mydworth are rallying round!"

"Glad to hear it," said Kat.

And with a nod, they left.

OUTSIDE IN the square, they stood together. Harry saw the last of the stalls being packed away, boys pushing handcarts piled high, and horses and vans manoeuvring around each other.

"So – um – what do you think? Instincts and all that?" he said.

"I think we have to get involved."

"Good. So do I. Plan of action?"

He knew that with Kat's experience working for a criminal lawyer back in New York, she'd be the voice to listen to here.

But also, in recent months he'd now seen first-hand how good she was at getting at the truth.

"How about I go see Mrs Buckman?"

"Right. And I could drop into the King's Arms, catch the gossip," he said, looking over at the crowded pub where drinkers were beginning to spill out onto the street. "*Vox populi*, as the emperors said."

"Give it an hour or so after my visit and I'd bet that *lot* will be even more talkative," said Kat.

"Oh, yes. Okay then… I know! I'll drop in on good old Sergeant Timms. Then meet in an hour for a pint?"

"Perfect," said Kat. "I *do* like being married to you."

"Fun, so far, isn't it?" said Harry. He doffed his hat to her and headed off to the police station.

3.

A POACHER'S LIFE

Kat walked down the narrow street that led from the dress shop and the main square, following the signs to the station.

And when a gaunt man directing a pot-bellied horse and wagon tried to pass, she had to press tight against a nearby door frame, barely allowing the slow-moving wagon to pass her, rattling slowly on the cobblestone lane as if it was about to fall apart.

The man, eyes nearly hidden under cap, didn't look anywhere but straight ahead.

Guess, she thought, *that's what you do here. Man directs his cart in your direction, best move briskly… and make way!*

Far cry from her memory of the last time she was in her old neighbourhood, the Bronx's Grand Concourse suddenly *filled* with cars. Horses and wagons and carriages of all kinds… all beginning to vanish in the face of an assault by the affordable and – supposedly – reliable Ford Model T.

And with the wagon having passed, she headed down Station Road, away from the centre of the town proper, towards the bridge over the river, and the railway station.

Just before the bridge, down a half-hidden turning, she found Briar Lane – the home of the Buckmans.

She passed a few tiny cottages. With every step these homes seemed to grow smaller. Coming to what looked like a dead end to the dirt road, she saw the last – and smallest – cottage. No name on the gate, but it was as Nicola had described it.

EVEN FROM the outside, the word "ramshackle" hardly did the place justice.

The outside wood: splintery, blistering; well past the stage where a quick coat of paint could rescue it.

A miniscule front garden, of sorts, where a few flowering shrubs did battle with brown vines poised to take over.

A scattering of flagstones, looking randomly placed, led to the front door. Less of a path than a half-hearted collection of stones.

It was mid-morning, the sun warm, and a dead boy's mother waited inside.

Am I up to this? Kat wondered.

But no time for doubt, she knew, and she knocked on the shabby door three times.

THE WOMAN who opened the door was the picture of someone in grief.

Her entire face sagged, as if unable to fight gravity or the pain; her eyes, puffy and red from crying. That crying, for a mother, had to be near constant, day in and day out, as she waited for the terrible pain to somehow – *please God* – lessen.

In one hand, Elsie Buckman held the door open, perhaps using it for support. In the other hand, a cloth napkin, tightly twisted and braided around her fingers.

In the Mid-East, Kat had seen women, veiled, holding a string of beads tightly. Worry beads, her station chief had explained. "*See that, and you know that they have something to worry about… or grieve.*"

"Mrs Buckman?"

The woman's lower lip trembled just a bit, as if she had gotten out of the habit of actually speaking.

"Nicola Green asked me to, um, pop around." The woman looked confused.

Kat hurried to add more: "To talk to you about…" A hesitation here, but the next words absolutely necessary for this conversation. "Your son." *Did a new pearly tear suddenly form in the corner of each eye?* "About what happened."

The woman released the door. Stepped back, her face still looking so confused and tortured.

"D-do come in," the small, round woman said, backing up as if opening the gateway to a grand manor house instead of what was – it would soon become clear – a hovel.

ELSIE BUCKMAN had gestured to one of three chairs at a round wooden table that sat beside the smallest of cooking areas.

A single oil lamp added to the morning sunlight that did its best to dispel the gloominess of the house.

A dirt-brown easy chair squatted atop a rug with frayed edges. Most of the uncovered floor showed wide floorboards, with big gaps, probably with years of dirt and mud trapped within those too-wide openings.

Kat took the chair, doing her best to put the woman at ease.

"You're the American. His wife. But Miss Green said that—"

The woman's confused about why I'm here on my own.

"My husband… he is also looking into things, Mrs Buckman."

"Oh—"

The woman's face suddenly animated.

"Please, call me Elsie." Then, as if remembering what was actually happening here, she added, "M'lady."

Probably pointless to suggest that a simple "Kat" would do.

Then, the woman looked around her so-small cottage as if she had just been planted there in error.

"Ah, sorry – some tea perhaps? I can get the kettle going in no time at all."

Kat didn't feel as if she really wanted any tea.

Instead she said: "That would be nice."

The woman turned, the cloth in her hand gripped tight enough to be bandaging an unseen wound. The fingers free though as she lit the narrow gas stove, which came to life with a *whoosh.*

A tap turned on; coughing as it sputtered out water.

Kettle on, the mother finally turned back. Even this simple process had spoken of the woman's pain, Kat thought.

TEA WAS served in a pair of courtly cups featuring men in stockings twirling a woman in full gown and pompadour this way and that, in some idyllic meadow scene.

Probably the sweetest thing in the cottage, Kat thought. The woman sat opposite her at the tiny kitchen table.

"Elsie," said Kat, "Nicola said that you don't *believe* that your son's death" – the word, like a physical slap spoken in the mother's presence – "was an accident?"

Kat had brought out her small notebook as she asked the question, not knowing if there was anything here to be learned or not.

A LITTLE NIGHT MURDER

The woman's face changed – the droopy pouches that were cheeks, the eyes that seemed barely able to remain open – took on an unexpected animation.

"Accident? No, not an accident! My son, my Syd… Somebody had it in for him, I know it!"

Elsie leaned across the table, her eyes burning into Kat's.

"This… *somebody*," said Kat, "was it a person that Syd knew? Somebody that you know?"

Kat watched Elsie carefully as these words seemed to sink slowly in.

"Know?" she said, her shoulders drooping again. "I don't… It's just…"

Maybe there's no mystery here at all, thought Kat. *Maybe this is just a poor grieving mother, desperate for a different truth.*

Then the woman seemed to find a focus again.

"Two months ago, it all started," said Elsie. "Syd… he'd been going out more and more since the spring, you see. Out most nights. All night long. But he was bringing home a good bit of money he was, paying his share…"

"And you didn't ask him where that money was coming from."

"Oh, I knew all right. Same game as my Billy all these years. But Syd – he was after more'n just rabbits."

"You knew he was poaching deer."

Elsie shrugged.

"So what happened? Did people come round – tell him to stop? Threaten him?"

"Hmm? No. Nothing like that. Just… he started to get all jumpy. Listening out all the time. Hearing noises outside. Nerves, like. I asked him what was up, and he said… He said… someone had it in for him. I asked him who. But he just went all quiet on me, told me to mind my own."

"This is all useful Elsie. Very useful," said Kat nodding. She made a note in her notebook. "Tell me, did anything else happen in the last couple of months? Anything... unusual?"

"Unusual?" said Elsie. "No, nothing unusual. Though... Syd did go away for a couple of days."

"Away? Where to?"

"I don't know. He put on his good shirt, had a wash. Went off. On the train it was. Came back next day."

"He ever do that before?"

"Lord no. Maybe out boozing all night. But not going away proper somewhere."

"When was this?"

"Oh, June some time. Beginning of June."

"And how was he when he came back?"

"Funny you ask that. He was cheery, he was. Dead cheery. Like the cat that got the cream." .

And Kat was about to ask more about this mysterious trip when – at the other end of the kitchen area – a door popped open.

A man walked in, hoisting one of his denim overall straps back into place, licking his lips, face specked with black and grey stubble, but his head nearly bald with only thin wisps jutting left and right.

Elsie turned. She radiated a sudden tension that Kat could feel.

And even from here, Kat caught the whiff of alcohol emanating from the man.

From Elsie's husband.

And Syd Buckman's father.

"*WOT?*" THE MAN said, still struggling to get that strap into place.

From the look of things Kat could guess where the man had been. Outside.

House like this, well, indoor plumbing was a luxury well beyond their dreams.

"Billy, this is the woman that Nicola…"

"*That* one."

Billy Buckman shook his head. Just based on appearances, Kat guessed a man like this would have little respect for something like the WVS and its services for women.

"Lot of good *any* of this will do… and hang on! Where's the other one? Mr High and Mighty? The one who's s'*posed* to be so clever?"

Billy had actually taken steps closer. This place clearly his domain.

And while Kat tended to reserve judgement on people – a useful policy especially when one travelled the world, representing one's government – in this case she would make an *exception*. She did not like this man, this drunk. *One bit.*

"Mr Buckman, Sir Harry and I are trying to help you," as she said that last word, she looked at Elsie, "about your son. The accident."

Billy took another step as if these were fighting words. He raised a hand, and pointed a finger right at Kat.

Yup, definitely do not like this man, she thought.

"Tell you *wot.* You're a Yank, right? That *accident* was just that. An accident. And we don't need your bloody meddling." Billy Buckman snorted, a bullish gesture apparently designed to emphasise the point he was making. "You hear that, now, don't you?"

Again – that finger, aimed at Kat like a gun.

Lot of things I could do, Kat thought. *Including leave.*

34

But then Elsie spoke.

"M'lady." The mother shot a glance at her wobbly husband as if reminding him just who sat at their tawdry table.

And now, perhaps a case of old habits dying hard, Billy nodded. Summoned a bit of sheepishness. "All right. All right. Thing is, *we've* been so upset here. B—but I can tell you why I know… *wot* I know."

Kat nodded. "That would be good."

Another snort. Then Billy stepped over to a cabinet above the sink, and pulled down a bottle of amber liquid. A half-full bottle of whisky, that he opened, and poured into a glass.

Kat watched as Elsie now bristled with tension, her eyes narrowed, looking at her husband.

The whole posture, the gaze speaking of… fear.

Fear of her husband.

Billy took a swig of the booze. Licked his lips.

And began to speak. Slowly. Carefully.

As if to make sure he said exactly what he wanted to, no more, no less.

"I knew my lad was out poachin'," said Billy, his hand wrapped around the glass of whisky. "See, that's where… yes… where he must have got the money he walked around with."

He nodded as if that explanation made perfect sense.

"Been bagging himself a lot of them deer. Fetching good prices too! That's what it was. Elsie – isn't that right?"

Kat quickly swivelled to look at the wife, body positioned the same. Eyes still narrowed to worried slits.

But now her lips, which had been pursed, moved.

"I… I.…"

Billy waited. And an unspoken threat hung in the air.

And Kat had to wonder, *How brutal could this drunk of a husband be?*

A LITTLE NIGHT MURDER

And as Billy's rheumy eyes locked on Elsie, the woman nodded. Two… three quick jerky nods – but not turning to look at Kat as if to really affirm that she agreed.

Because she didn't.

Billy was lying right now.

He took another big glug of the whisky. Refill time coming soon.

"But here's the thing. I told the boy… standing right here… told him time and time again… that even with all his training, what I gave him… you got to be careful with guns. Even the best of 'em can make a mistake. Terrible thing…"

A slow, dramatic shake of his head, and Kat ever more convinced that the father of the dead boy was lying again.

"That's what took our boy. Bit of carelessness, a stumble, and well…"

And now Billy turned to Kat, his face brightening, either at the fact he had concluded his successful deception… or from the ruddy burn of the alcohol.

"There you go. Sad to say. An accident."

And from Billy's look, she guessed he expected her to leave. All the facts – as fabricated by Syd's father – on the table. Elsie silenced.

And that was the thing that most worried her… the woman, trapped with this man.

But Kat *wasn't* done.

Time to see how Billy stood up under some more difficult questions.

"MR BUCKMAN, I actually need to ask you about something else."

Billy's forced smile evaporated and he shook his head.

"Told you – *we* told you – all we know. That's it. You understan'?"

Kat nodded.

"Um, yes. I'm sure you think that's it. But what do you know about the threats?"

And here Kat was hesitant. Would this next sentence make the poor woman's life harder?

"The threats against your son…"

She looked at Elsie but the woman, a stone figure now, didn't turn and look at her.

"Threats against his life, Mr Buckman. You must know about those?"

And now, for a completely different reason, Billy paused before speaking. Finishing the tumbler of alcohol. Then, with a bang, slamming the filmy glass down on the small counter space near their sink,

"*Listen…* sounds like you don't hear too good. Is that a problem with you Yanks? Don't listen? Don't hear? I told you what we know. And we don't know nothin' about any threats."

"And what about the trip that Syd took last June? I suppose you know nothing about that either?"

"Trip? I don't know nothing about no *trip*."

And then Billy took a step towards Kat, a wobbly step but not so wobbly that his barrel shape and meaty fists didn't seem to pose a danger.

"You can get out of here. Now. Leave us the hell be," then with a smirk, "m'lady. We still got laws in this country, you know? *My* house. I can have who I *wants* in it, or not."

And, at that, Kat stood up, glad to be a good number of inches taller than Billy.

Wondering also what it would be like to push back against the bullying goon.

She looked over to Elsie who only now had turned.

And she directed her words strictly at Syd's mother.

"Thanks. And I'll let *you* know if we find out anything."

The slightest of nods from the woman, as Kat turned and walked out of the shabby cottage, the air now thick with anger and alcohol.

4.

A CALL ON THE SERGEANT

Harry took the few stone steps up to the small police station, home to Sergeant Timms and his constables.

A place he'd never been to before.

That alone made this all rather… *interesting.*

He opened the door, and entered to see Timms, in uniform, sitting at his desk.

Reading a newspaper.

Yup. Crime doesn't have a chance here, Harry thought.

Timms looking up, and seeing Harry, shot to his feet. Or at least as much of a "shot" as the portly officer could perform.

"Sir Harry! Is everything all right? Not a problem at the manor house, I hope?"

Harry was almost tempted to tell the man "at ease".

"No – all good there, Sergeant Timms. Lady Lavinia sends her regards."

At this falsehood, Timms beamed.

Harry put a hand to his chin. "There's a little… matter… I need to speak to you about."

Timms eyebrows raised.

"A *matter?*"

"Yes," Harry said, smiling, hoping to disarm the momentary ripple of alarm that his words had created.

Timms gestured to a simple wooden chair that faced his desk. "Care to sit and we can discuss this matter of yours, sir?"

"No, thank you, Sergeant, I'm quite good standing. Won't be long but, you see, I had a few questions. About Syd Buckman."

And Timms – doing his best to play catch-up with Harry's words – made an oval shape with his lips, a near theatrical expression, especially when topped by Timms' carefully maintained moustache.

"The lad who had the accident?"

"That very one. You see, his mother, poor dear, asked me and my wife, well, to look into it." Another grin. "Seems after all that business we did for my aunt, well, we now have a bit of reputation all of a sudden."

"I see," Timms said, not with any great deal of confidence. "The mother must be hit hard. Distraught."

"I imagine. Father too."

At those words Timms' eyes narrowed.

"Billy Buckman? *That* one? Well, maybe in those rare moments when he's sober. Rare indeed, sir."

"Bit of a drinker? Anyway, I had a few questions, about the accident – I mean you being the expert and all that."

Must be careful not to overplay this, Harry thought. *Even Timms might be able to tell when he's being – in fact – interrogated.*

"You determined quite clearly that it was an accident?"

"Oh, yes. Lad was poaching. Found red-handed with a young deer. Must have tripped and—"

"Gun went off, hmm?"

"Precisely. Cut his head on the way down too."

"I'd think though – wouldn't you, Sergeant? – a man used to hunting, at night… he'd normally be pretty careful. Unless, like his father, that night, he was also in his cups?"

But Timms shook his head. "Would have been my guess as well, sir. But no. Not a whiff of drink about him. No flask to keep the night chill away. Stone-cold sober, I'd say."

"And yet… somehow stone-cold dead. Tripped, fell… his finger on the trigger?"

Timms nodded with admirable certitude.

"Do you think, Sergeant – just curious – I could take a look at the rifle? That is, if you still have it?"

"Certainly can, sir, certainly can."

Timms started moving to a back room.

"Locked up, nice and tidy." A look back to Harry as if he'd understand. "It is evidence, after all."

"That it is," Harry said.

Moments later, Timms returned, cradling the rifle, barrel pointing down.

HARRY IMMEDIATELY noticed a reddish smear at the end of the barrel. At least Timms hadn't tampered with the weapon. Syd Buckman's blood stain was still in place.

Harry scanned the rifle, so familiar from his service days, pulled back the bolt, opened the chamber, removed the magazine, replaced it, looked down the sight. Then he examined the stock.

"No serial number," he said to Timms.

"Sanded off, sir. No surprise there, lot of guns like this came back from France, ended up in attics, cellars. Or poachers' hands."

"Good weapon. Perfect for taking down a deer, I imagine. But there is one thing about this, Sergeant…"

"Yes?"

"The safety – on a Lee Enfield?"

Harry clicked it off and on.

"No mistaking having that on. Or off. Nicely placed, right? Flick of the thumb. You'd need to actually have to make a decision to *not* put it on, or likewise, keep the safety off."

"Maybe he hadn't put it on yet?"

Harry turned to Timms and stated the obvious.

Which for the sergeant might not exactly be so obvious.

"But, as you said, he had bagged a deer. The hunting – the poaching – for that night was over. Flick the safety on, and you head home. That – or remove all the rounds from the magazine. And yet, you think that's *not* what happened?"

Harry thought he saw a hint on the officer's face that, somewhere inside his head, a light bulb had just flickered on.

"Well, sir, I imagine, um, well, yes… that *is* a bit odd, now that you mention it. Still—"

Timms quick retreated to his favoured theory.

"The most reasonable explanation, all things considered, is – plain and simple – an *accident*."

Harry wasn't convinced that Timms had – as he mentioned – considered *all things*.

He handed the officer back the rifle.

A nod, as Harry took time for his next question. Timms was a good, cooperative sort – so far. But Harry was aware it would not be impossible to have the man retreat to a more official and bureaucratic stance, leaving Harry with no answers to his next questions.

Such as…

"Syd Buckman. You knew he went out, poached?"

"Well, sir, it was more or less common knowledge. Runs in the family, so it does. His dad Billy's record's as long as my arm. Petty stuff, to be sure. But we here – me and the constables – don't have the resources to go traipsing through the woods looking for such people."

"Of course you don't," Harry quickly agreed.

"But, yes, we knew what Syd was up to."

"And so – I'm guessing – did the landowner Mr Shreeve."

Was that another thought that hadn't occurred to the sergeant? *Could easily be…*

"Oh, I imagine he would have. I mean, his property, his deer. His estate manager must have been alert to the problem. Regular patrols, and what have you."

"But you're not sure of that?"

A headshake.

"No. Did not occur to me to ask."

"But you *did* talk to the estate manager? Now, what's his name – Nailor – that right?"

"Yes, sir, Fred Nailor. That I did. It was Fred found the body."

"Ah, I see. That must have been hard on him."

"All part of the job, I suppose," said Timms, clearly not having considered that.

"And the deer?"

"Sir?"

"What happened to the deer, Sergeant?"

"Why, sir, I returned it to its rightful owner Mr Shreeve. He came down here to the station next day, once we'd finished with it."

Harry nodded. "And how did he seem to feel… about the boy's death, this accident? Upset or…?"

Timms shook his head. "Can't rightly say. Fred Nailor was with him. He took the sack with the deer, put it in his van. Mr Shreeve himself thanked me." A pause. "Though he did mutter something – excuse the language, sir – 'damned poachers', he said."

"A problem these days, is it? Poachers?"

"Well, you know how it is, sir. Lot of large estates in the area. Can't be many locals never tasted a pheasant? Turned a blind eye to how it ended up on their plate."

"But deer – that's a different game, hmm?"

"Oh yes. Serious offence, that is. Only one or two locals go for the deer. But there's a few more bad'uns like Buckman further out on the Downs. Also some right dodgy types, itinerants, wandering from village to village. Probably – in the long run – safer for them that way."

Harry smiled. "Sergeant, thank you so much. Most helpful to understand exactly what" – careful choice of words here – "might have happened. One last thing…"

Timms sniffed, a gentle bracing for whatever next unexpected question was about to pop up.

"If somehow – I know it's unlikely – it wasn't an accident, are you aware of anyone who had a grudge against Syd Buckman?"

"Not to my knowledge, sir. I mean we haven't gone around asking about that particular subject."

Harry nodded as if that was perfectly all right.

"Yes. No real reason. Accident and all that. But if you do happen to learn anything, or think of someone who might have had an issue with the lad… do you think – I mean, all probably nothing – that you might ring me with the name?"

"Absolutely, sir. Though I have to say—"

"Good man, Sergeant." Harry pulled out a notebook and roughly tore out a sheet of paper from it.

"Here's my phone number at the Dower House. Maybe, just keep it close. Should anything pop up."

"Right, right, sir. Oh – there is one thing. The boy's father?"

"Yes?"

"Keeps coming around demanding his property back."

"Property?"

"The rifle, sir. I explained to him that it was evidence. Must stay locked up until the matter is *fully* settled. Shouldn't be long. But I must say he's rather belligerent about it. Had to give him a bit of a warning."

"I see. That is odd. Worried more about the rifle than his son?"

"Yes. Sort of… seemed so."

Harry started for the door out, then stopped, turning.

"Thanks again, Sergeant. You've been most helpful."

And at that, the sergeant, chest puffed up, smiled right back.

5.

TWO HALF PINTS AT THE KING'S ARMS

Kat had waited for Harry outside the pub, the afternoon warm enough to make standing outside perfect.

There was also the fact that she hadn't been in this pub yet. The protocol with this most British institution… a little intimidating. But then she saw Harry dash across the square and run right up to her.

He quickly put a hand to her shoulder.

"Ready to brave the King's Arms? I mean, we could go to the tea room, though that place tends to get a bit crowded on a nice day like this. Or we could——"

"The pub. About time, don't you think?"

"Right, exactly. Okay then, well – in we go!"

And he led the way to the heavy wooden door, with multi-coloured glass panels, all bevelled, hiding the wonders of whatever was inside.

HARRY STOPPED just a few feet in, and turned to Kat.

"So, how about you go get us a nice table in the snug there——"

He pointed to a little ante-room that quite obviously was segregated from the main arena of the pub itself.

"I think," Kat said slowly, "maybe we just stand at the bar, hmm? For our little catch-up?"

Did she know that what she was suggesting was far from the norm for a woman visiting the King's Arms?

Of course she does, Harry thought.

Nonetheless, he tried a bit of dissuasion.

"Well, you see, *Lady Mortimer*, that lovely little room over there is expressly designed for…"

Kat fired another quick glance to where Harry was pointing, and then turned back.

"I know. Can figure that out. The snug is where the womenfolk sit?"

"Right. That, um, is the general idea."

And she took a step closer to Harry. Very close, he noted, her voice a whisper, her lips…

Well, *close as well.*

"You see, *Sir Harry*, I used to tend a bar. Just like this one here. I have no need of little wooden tables with tiny lamps and their shades with dangling tassels."

"I *see*." And he did. "Okay, then. How about, as you Americans say, we belly up to the bar?"

And he took her hand, and walked her to the great wooden bar of the King's Arms.

AS SOON as they were there, Kat felt the few patrons sitting at nearby tables, all men, kind of old, looking like they might live here, nursing pints from the looks of things, eyeing exactly *what* was going on here.

To which Kat decided to pay no attention.

But the barman, a barrel-chested fellow with dark eyes and a bushy salt and pepper beard came over.

Harry turned from the barman, then back to her.

"Kat, I want you to meet an old friend of mine, the proprietor of this establishment, Johnny Fox."

For a moment, Kat couldn't tell whether the Falstaffian bar owner was scrutinising her or just preparing an appropriate greeting.

"Well, well. Sir Harry, you didn't tell me that your American bride was *this* beautiful."

Now Johnny Fox's face burst into a broad smile.

"Not only that, Johnny – smart too."

Johnny nodded. "Lady Mortimer." Johnny said, still smiling at Kat with a look that said *any friend of Harry's…*

And Kat smiled back. "Think, if I'm to become a regular here… maybe just Kat?"

"Ha! Kat it is!" Then, leaning close. "Now, what can I get for the two of *yers?*"

"Two half pints of mild I think." Harry looked at Kat as though she actually understood what he was saying. "Sound about right, Kat?"

She laughed at that. "Sure," as Johnny Fox went down to the other end of the bar to fill the order.

"SO, THOSE words you just said: 'half-pint of mild?'"

"Oh, well, I think perhaps it's a bit early in the day for a full pint."

"Bit early for any beer, period, in my opinion."

"Touché," said Harry. "But when in Rome…"

"And mild?"

"Pretty run of the mill English beer. You don't have it in the colonies?"

Kat had to grin at that. At her father's bar, she'd served lots of different beer and ales. No one had ever ordered a "mild" though.

"This'll be a first. Still acclimating, you see."

"And doing jolly well at that too."

"Okay, pretty quiet at the bar. Guess it might be a good spot to talk, share what we learned?"

"Oh yes. I had a most interesting chat with Sergeant Timms."

Johnny Fox came back, placing the two small glasses of beer on coasters.

She picked up a glass. A sip.

"Warm," she said when the barman was out of earshot.

"Well, yes. I mean, why would you ever chill a beer?"

"Have to tell you, Harry – or, better yet, show you some day – the wonders of say, an afternoon at Yankee Stadium. Watching the great Lou Gehrig at bat, with a hot dog in your hand, on a really warm summer day. And the beer? Icy cold."

"You *do* paint a picture." He clinked his glass to hers. "So Timms," he said. "He's totally convinced it was an accident, despite all evidence to the contrary."

"Such as?"

"The rifle, for one. Lee Enfield."

"Not up to date on my firearms. Important because?"

"The safety. It's no out-of-the-way latch. You'd know it was on, and 'on' it would stay unless you were ready to shoot."

"But Syd Buckman had already –"

"*Precisely.* Bagged his deer. Heading home. If he knew his way around the weapon – as any good poacher would – it would be barrel pointed down, safety on, and magazine empty. Oh, and by the way, not to get too, um, detailed here, the barrel had a broad smear of Syd's blood."

"But that wouldn't be unusual – would it? Kinda what you'd expect in a hunting accident, surely. Where was the entry wound?"

"Chest, I think."

"So that fits with a fall. The boy trips, lurches forward onto the gun, finger pulls on the trigger…"

Harry took another slow sip of beer. "Nasty head wound too, according to Timms."

"So – Syd smashed his head on the ground when he fell?"

"Hmm," said Harry. "Sounds like you _do_ think it was an accident."

"Just looking at all the angles. But you're not subscribing to Timms' theory then?"

"No, I still don't."

"Good. Cause wait till you hear what I learned."

"Now see, this is getting really fun. And here I thought I was bringing you back to a sleepy little town in Sussex."

"Oh, there's nothing sleepy about Mydworth," said Kat, putting her empty half-pint glass back on the counter. "Fact – I think I'm going to need the other 'half' while I tell you about the home life of the Buckman family."

And Harry watched as Kat summoned Johnny and ordered two more halves of mild…

6.

SYD'S SECRET

Harry nodded as he listened to his wife talk through her conversation with Elsie and Billy Buckman. When she'd finished, he leaned back, looked at her. Her face – something that he doubted he'd ever get tired of looking at – had turned serious. Eyes dark, piercing.

"The poor mother, Harry. Like she was trapped by her husband."

"I know the type. And if he ever threatened you…"

Kat smiled at that. "Oh, I think it's well within my abilities to deal with the likes of Billy Buckman."

And Harry laughed back.

"That old left hook?"

"You got it. Followed by a jab to the body."

"Ouch!" said Harry, laughing.

Harry took a sip of his beer. "What Elsie said, though. Interesting. Could Syd's little trip away be connected to these threats?"

"Maybe. I didn't get a chance to find out more. Billy shut up shop when I asked."

"But you felt he was lying?"

"Yeah. No question. He's hiding something."

Harry looked away. Not for the first time he thought – well – the two of them, despite their experiences abroad, working for king and country, were not *really* detectives.

So, all this confused him. *What could Billy Buckman be hiding? And why?*

And then an even more bizarre notion, *What if he had something to do with his son's accident?*

"Penny for your thoughts," Kat said.

Harry shook his head, grinning. "Oh, not sure they're worth even that! It's just, the two of us, we don't seem to have a clue what's going on."

"Yet."

"I do like your confidence."

"Things will come together, Harry."

Harry looked down at the other end of the bar – Johnny busying himself polishing glasses.

But the barman saw Harry look over. He put down the towel and walked over.

"Another round, Sir Harry?"

"'Fraid not, Johnny. But I was wondering. You see, Kat and I… we've been helping Elsie Buckman. Trying to put her mind at rest."

"Bad business, that. Poor woman."

"Yeah." Harry looked at Kat, wondering if she could guess what he was about to ask.

"Syd Buckman ever come in here?"

"Sure. From time to time."

"And seemed to have the funds?"

"For a few beers? Didn't have a problem. Certainly not recently."

Harry glanced at Kat. *Recently…*

Then back at Johnny: "People knew what he was up to? The poaching. I mean?"

At that, Johnny hesitated. "Who didn't? But – well – a man's business is a man's business, right? So, the lad nabbed a little extra to put on the table now and then. No love lost between a *lot* of my patrons here and the big landowners. Most of them, that is."

Harry smiled at that. "I'm sure my aunt will be glad to hear she's excluded."

"That she is, Harry. Big heart there. But you know that."

Then, a question from Kat – showing that she was riding the same train as he was: "Johnny… any problems with Syd? Fights or arguments?"

The barman looked away. "Well, not in here, in my place, I can tell you. None that I saw."

Harry sensed Johnny had more to say on the subject.

"But there were some?"

"Had a bit of a short fuse on him, did Syd," said Johnny.

"So, outside, after closing?"

"Maybe. The odd disagreement… come to blows."

"Anything particular? In the last month or so?" said Kat.

"I did hear he had a run-in with someone out in the square a few weeks back. Word was, another poacher fella. But, like I said, wasn't in here." Johnny smiled. "My customers know that."

Harry looked over at Kat. *A fight with another poacher.* She nodded.

"And any mates he'd come in here with?"

Johnny Fox scratched his thick beard. "Well, you know the young folk. Just sort of lolly-gagging together. Not sure… well, no… hang on now. I think, yes, he did have one friend that he seemed close to. Chaz Todd."

Harry saw Kat shoot him a smile.

A friend. Syd's mate. And a name.

Useful indeed.

"And," Harry followed up with, "happen to know where we'd find him?"

"Do indeed. Works with his dad, the blacksmith. Has his forge up on Hill Lane. Pretty much serves as the farrier, least for the regular folk. Chaz is learning the trade. Imagine you'll find him there most days."

"Thanks Johnny," said Harry, looking at Kat. Then an afterthought: "By the way, you ever get people from the Shreeve Estate in here?"

"One or two. Come in for a pint, now and then."

"How about Fred Nailor?"

"Fred? He pops in. Fact, that's him now," Harry saw Johnny turn and nod to the rear of the pub, where two men were draining their pints and putting them back on the bar. "Over there. Big fella with the moustache. You want a word?"

"Quick chat."

Johnny nodded and went down the bar.

Harry saw him lean towards the two men. One of them, tall, moustache, forties, looked up the bar to Harry and Kat, patted his companion on the shoulder and walked through the pub towards them.

"Mr Nailor?" said Harry, rising from his bar stool and offering a hand. "Harry Mortimer... my wife Kat."

"Pleasure," said Nailor, shaking both their hands. "What can I do for you?"

Harry smiled at the man, liking his attitude already. He had an easy manner, and a warm handshake.

"I don't want to bother you now – but we'd like to chat with you sometime about the young man found up on the estate a couple of weeks back?"

Harry saw Nailor's face darken. "Terrible thing that was. Boy losing his life like that." Nailor took a breath. "Must have devastated his poor mum... can't imagine..."

"I know," said Harry.

Nailor leaned close. "It's the stupidity of it that angers me. I *know* times are hard, but messing about with guns, poaching?"

He stopped, shaking his head. Then looked up at Harry. "But, why are you...?"

"We've been asked by friends of the family to find out what we can about what might have happened," said Kat.

Harry saw Nailor nod. "Ah. Put their minds at rest? That the kind of thing?"

"Something like that," said Harry. He softened his voice, leaned in: "King's Arms not really the place, though, to discuss this. Is there somewhere a little more...?"

"Of course," said Nailor. "I'm just heading back up to the estate now. Should be finished by six. Why don't you drop by the estate office, have a cup of tea?"

"Perfect," said Harry. "Appreciate your understanding, Mr Nailor."

"Grieving family," said Nailor. "We all do what we can, don't we?"

"Exactly," said Harry.

"I'd best be off," said Nailor, tipping his hat to Kat. "Nice to meet you both."

"And you," said Kat.

Nailor waved to his pal down the bar, and, with a "cheers, Johnny", headed out of the pub.

"Looks like we've got a busy afternoon," said Kat.

"Right enough," said Harry, and he went to pull out his wallet as Johnny came over.

"Sorry, Harry," said Johnny, eyeing the wallet. "First visit with the missus? This one's on me."

Harry caught Kat's eye and grinned: *the missus.*

There were a good number of things he'd missed about Mydworth.

And Johnny was one of them.

STANDING OUTSIDE the pub, a few feet away from the great wooden door and the shade of the building so that the perfectly warm afternoon sun hit them, Kat asked Harry, "Time to visit the friend? This Chaz?"

"Yup. If anyone is going to know something about Syd, it would be his best pal."

"Everyone has secrets," Kat said.

She well knew that from her work for her country abroad.

At the same time, everyone needs someone to share those secrets with.

"Shall we go together?" Harry said. "Then head over to the Shreeve Estate, end of the day?"

"Think so. All this, is getting – well, to quote one of your country's authors – *curiouser…*"

"*And* curiouser. Agree. But one thing, Kat. And it may have occurred to you already."

She saw Harry's deep blue eyes, catching the light. His black hair, needing a bit of a trim, blowing with the gentle breeze.

"If Syd Buckman's death *was* no accident, then we need to be aware of one thing."

He didn't have to finish the sentence. She nodded.

"That – there is a killer, somewhere out there. Loose. Thinking they got away with it."

"Yes. And maybe," he lowered his voice, "none too happy about," he gestured with his hand as if stirring a large, invisible pot, "what we're up to."

"You talking about danger, Sir Harry?"

"I do believe I am, Lady Mortimer."

And she smiled. "Duly noted. Now let's find Syd's friend."

And they set off across the square and up the High Street, past the row of shops, to the small lane with a blacksmith's forge at the end.

7.

MATES NO MORE

Kat could hear the clanging sounds of the blacksmith's, and smell the acrid metallic smoke from the forge, long before they reached the end of Hill Lane.

"One thing that doesn't change, the world over," she said, glancing at Harry who strode next to her.

"Horses still need shoes, hmm? So much for modern times," said Harry, as they pushed open the gate to the yard. Kat could see old cartwheels, bits of farm machinery, a great pile of coke, gates, stacked tools – and a pair of shire horses tied to a rail, presumably waiting to be shod.

The door to the forge itself was open, and inside she saw figures moving, shadows flickering in the light of the fire as hammer blows rang out. She stepped into the doorway, Harry behind her. As she peered in, the blast of heat in the small shed was intense, fierce as it hit her face.

Two men, stripped to the waist, stood working together over an anvil, a red-hot length of metal smoking and sizzling between them as they shifted it with great callipers: a young man – dark-haired, sweat pouring from him – held the metal still, as the other man – fifties, bald, ox-like – pounded holes into the glowing metal with some kind of chisel and a hammer.

Neither of them looked up, but they both seemed to sense Kat and Harry's arrival.

Harry looked at Kat, then, raising his voice over the din of clanging metal and the fiery gasps of the furnace, said, "You think we could have a word?"

The older man, obviously the owner, didn't even look up from the searing hot metal.

"Got these shoes to finish up. Talk in the yard," he shouted back at them.

"Absolutely," said Harry, nodding to Kat – and she followed him back outside into the fresh summer air to wait.

TEN MINUTES later, Harry saw the two men emerge, carrying the finished sets of horseshoes, hanging them on nails by the horses.

As the younger man dipped his hands into a large trough of water and washed his face, the blacksmith turned and walked over.

"Mr Todd?" said Harry.

"Aye, that's me," said the smithy.

"Harry Mortimer."

"I know who you are," said Todd, wiping his hands on a cloth. "Shod horses for your family when you were a nipper."

At that moment, Todd, seeming as tough as the hot metal he worked with, seemed to pause.

Harry thought, *This man knew my parents. And right now, for a moment, I'm not just some landed gentry interrupting his work.*

"What can I do for you?"

Harry smiled: "Afraid we've not brought any work."

The smithy stared for a second. "No? Nothing for your aunt?"

"Not that I am aware of. But my wife and I would like a word with your son, Chaz, if you'll allow us."

"He's his own man. You can ask him yourself," said Todd. He called over to the lad. "Chaz!"

Harry watched as the young man pulled a rough shirt over his head and walked over.

"Not in trouble, is he?" said Todd as Chaz joined him.

"No, not at all," said Harry. "Thought Chaz might be able to tell us a little bit about Syd Buckman."

"We're helping out Syd's family," said Kat.

"Do-gooders?" said Todd, spitting at the ground. Then he turned to Chaz.

"Five minutes. Then we'll start on the mare."

Chaz nodded obediently, and Harry watched as his father returned to the forge.

"Nothing to worry about, Chaz. Just a couple of questions," said Harry, smiling at the lad.

Chaz took tobacco and paper from his top pocket, rolled a cigarette in seconds and lit it with a flick of a match. "Like my dad said, five minutes."

He walked over to a stack of logs and sat, smoking, waiting for Kat and Harry to join him.

KAT SAW Harry give her the slightest of nods. She knew what that meant — *you lead.*

She smiled at Chaz. "We heard you and Syd were good friends."

Chaz shrugged.

"He was a mate."

"You knew him a long time?" said Kat.

"*Whaddya* think? Grew up in the same town, didn't we?"

"So — really good pals."

"I *suppose* so," Chaz laughed. "We drank together."

"Best pals, so we heard," said Harry.

Chaz's smirk vanished.

"Maybe at one time."

Kat watched him carefully. *Something here,* she thought. *Something bothering Chaz. But we have only five minutes to get at it…*

"But not recently."

Chaz shrugged again.

"You two fell out?" she said.

"Syd, well… he had other stuff to think about."

"Such as?" said Harry.

"I dunno. Didn't have much time for grabbing pints with me any more."

"When did that start to happen?" said Kat.

"Dunno. Maybe a couple of months back."

"So… June some time?" said Kat.

"Around then."

Interesting, thought Kat, with a quick glance to Harry. *Time to cut to the chase.*

"Mrs Buckman said… seemed he came into a bit of money," she said.

"Maybe," said Chaz. "Like I said… *dunno.*"

"Not all of it legal?"

"Look. Not sure what the two of yers are gettin' at, but I don't know nothing about that," said Chaz.

Time for a big one, she thought.

"You never went poaching with him?"

Kat watched Chaz take a final puff from his cigarette, pinch the end, and put it in his top pocket.

"Bloody hell. What's with all this? These questions. You helping the police?"

A LITTLE NIGHT MURDER

"No," said Kat.

"*Listen.* I stay out of trouble, I do. I'm happy here working with my dad. Got a job. *Proper* job."

"Of course," said Harry.

"Don't worry, Chaz," said Kat. "Trust us. Nothing you tell us is going to get you into trouble."

"Good, coz I ain't done *nothing* – got that?" said Chaz, looking over his shoulder at the forge where his dad was working, then back to them.

"Sure," said Kat. "We're just trying to find out what happened to Syd."

"These last two months," said Harry. "When Syd had money... I suppose he was out and about, drinking?"

"Too right! Drinking more than I could afford, that's for sure. Buying rounds and all that. Not just here in the town. He was off down to Portsmouth some nights. Brighton too. Having himself a grand old time."

"Had new friends, did he?" said Harry.

"Dunno about that. Like I said, hardly saw him any more."

"And travelling some, was he?" said Kat. "We heard he went away for a couple of days back in June. You remember that?"

Kat saw him shrug: "Maybe. Rings a bell."

"But you don't know where he went?"

"He didn't say." Chaz's irritation seemed to grow with each question, Kat noticed. "And I didn't ask!"

"But, apparently, he came back with money," said Harry. "Started spending then?"

Chaz seemed to think about this. "Not straight away. But... maybe soon after."

Kat looked at Harry. He nodded back. *Keep asking questions.*

"You must have been shocked, hmm?" said Kat. "When you heard he'd died?"

"Course."

"Were you surprised?"

"Bloody risk he took, wasn't it?"

"What? Poaching?" said Kat.

"*Not* poaching," said Chaz, wiping a shred of tobacco from his lips. "Wasn't 'poaching' that killed him. Going up into Shreeve's woods in the middle of the night – *that's* what killed him."

Kat paused, not sure what Chaz meant.

"Those woods dangerous?" said Harry. "How?"

"Hang on. You mean you two don't know what Shreeve did?"

"I'd like to hear it from you," said Harry quickly, a glance over at Kat revealing his excitement at this unexpected development.

"See, Shreeve had this big row with Syd, few Saturdays back. Market day it was. Pushed him around. Even said he'd horsewhip him if he ever saw him on his land again."

"Wait. Shreeve *knew* that Syd was poaching his deer?" said Kat.

"Chaz!" came a shout from the forge, and Kat turned to see Mr Todd appear.

Five minutes up so quickly, she thought.

Chaz got up and grabbed some tools from beside the logs.

And now Chaz's smirky grin returned.

"Wasn't just Shreeve's deer that Syd was poaching," said Chaz, shaking his head. "Was his precious daughter, that Melissa, wasn't it?"

"What?" said Harry.

Kat saw Chaz smile: "So if you lot want to know what happened to Syd - you talk to that bastard Shreeve."

And with that, he nodded a clear "goodbye" and walked across the yard to join his father by the horses. *Interview over.*

8.

FAMILY MAN

Harry wheeled the big old motorbike round to the front of the Dower House and waited for Kat.

They'd come back home for a late lunch – thick chunks of bread with ham, cheese and pickle – and now the plan was to head out to the Shreeve Estate to talk to Fred Nailor.

And maybe grab a minute with Arthur Shreeve himself.

Or even Shreeve's daughter Melissa.

If Chaz wasn't making all that up, thought Harry. *Just spinning yarns…*

The front door opened and Harry saw Kat appear – changed out of her brindle dress into overalls and short boots.

"Well, don't you look ready for a motorbike," he said, as she came over to the bike.

"Um, who's driving?" she said as he handed her a helmet and goggles.

He paused. *Was she joking? It was his bike after all, and… and…*

But he watched her expertly adjust her goggles and clip her helmet into place – like she'd done it a thousand times.

The question of "driver" clearly an open one.

"And there was me thinking I'd finally have something to be able to teach you," he said. "Some hope."

"Sorry, Harry. If it makes you feel any better – I know absolutely nothing about sail boats."

"Thank *God!* Maybe we should buy one? Keep it on the river!"

"How lovely! You can teach me, then we can sail all the way to the sea. Take a picnic."

"Why stop there? Weekend in France! Channel tides permitting!"

"Oh yes. A hotel romantique *sur la plage!*"

"*Exactement.* Kind of want to do that… right now." For a moment he held her gaze, lost in that rather delicious reverie. "Well, meanwhile, may I suggest – at least until people get to know you a little better – and you, the roads – that just this once, I drive?"

"Of course. I know how tender the male ego is on such subjects. And you did put her back together."

"Ah," he said, grinning, "it's not really my ego I'm protecting – it's the locals. I imagine if you drive a bike like you do a car, you'll strike the fear of God into them."

He sat on the bike and kick-started the motor, its satisfying growl low and easy. Behind him, Kat climbed onto the little extra seat, put her arms around him, leaned close.

"Let's go," she said, her lips close to his ear. "And don't spare the horsepower!"

He flicked the bike into gear, let out the throttle and off they went down the drive.

"Faster!" shouted Kat, her arms tight around Harry, as they blazed together over the Downs – the sea in the far distance a sparkling smear against the blue sky.

Five miles out of Mydworth, the road had straightened – a Roman road she guessed – and she could see from the speedo that Harry had them up to seventy.

Suddenly, all her fears that getting married and moving to England would mean tea parties, gardening, old ladies and stuffy conversations in grey dining rooms – all of *that* – seemed now to be blown away forever in the slipstream of this amazing motorbike.

Here she was, in the middle of what might well turn out to be a murder investigation, en route – at high speed, no less – to meet a suspect.

Yes, this is the life I wanted – the life I've always wanted.

"A bit faster?" she shouted again, and she gripped Harry tighter as he twisted the throttle and she felt the bike leap forward, past English fields and hedgerows under a sheer blue sky.

CRUISING DOWN the gravel drive to the Shreeve mansion, the house suddenly came into view, and Harry quickly realised just how wealthy Shreeve must be.

The mansion, which after the war was still owned by the elderly Lord and Lady Westland, had been on the verge of collapse last time he'd visited.

Now – under its new owner – it sparkled white, brilliant, with a new roof, stables, paddocks and what looked like a whole fleet of cars parked at the side.

The engine barely ticking over, they rolled closer, coasting at ten miles an hour, helmets and goggles off.

"Whoa. Quite the place," said Kat. "This Shreeve – he another of your local aristocrats?"

"Not at all," said Harry. "Factory owner. Moved down here with his family from the Midlands a few years ago."

"Dark satanic mills? Ill-gotten gains on the backs of the masses?"

"Not far off. Word is he had a buckle business. No big deal until 1914..."

"Ah – let me guess," said Kat. "War-time government contract?"

"Exactly. Ever count the buckles on a Tommy's uniform?"

"Every one a tidy profit, I'm sure."

"Made millions, apparently. Then sold up. Moved here."

"Guess I don't need to ask how you feel about all that?" said Kat.

No, thought Harry, remembering the horrors of the Western Front. *No, you don't.*

As they approached the forecourt, Harry saw a sign "Estate Office" pointing to the side of the house.

"Look," said Kat. "Up there at the corner."

Harry glanced up at the bedroom windows. A figure stood against the glass, staring out at them.

A girl in a yellow dress catching the sunlight – maybe a young woman. As he looked up, she quickly stepped back into darkness, as if nervous of being seen.

Was that Melissa? And, if so, could she really have been interested in Syd Buckman, poacher of these parts?

He turned off the engine, and Kat swung her leg neatly over and jumped off. Harry kicked out the parking rest and climbed off too.

"Nice ride, husband," she said, clipping her helmet to the bike.

A LITTLE NIGHT MURDER

Harry watched as she spun her loose hair round, took a grip from between her teeth, and deftly pinned it up in a neat bun.

"You're welcome," said Harry. "Next time – you're driving. And I get to hold you."

"Deal."

"All right, come on. Let's find Fred Nailor."

And they set off to look for the estate manager.

NAILOR WASN'T hard to find.

As they rounded the side of the mansion, Kat saw – just ahead – a small brick-built single-storey building with a tractor out front. Leaning against it, Fred Nailor was talking to a woman, while a little girl played at their feet.

The couple looked up as Kat and Harry approached.

"Sir Harry, Lady Mortimer," said Nailor. He put his hand gently on the woman's arm, propelling her forward. "My wife Rosie, and, the little'un, our Agnes."

Kat saw the woman was shy, uncertain, not sure how to greet them both; but the little girl was bolder.

"Hello," she said, peeping out from behind her mother's legs.

"Hello to you," said Kat, shaking the little girl's small hand, "how nice to meet *you*." She crouched down. "So, you're Agnes. What a nice name."

"Aggie," said the girl, beaming up at her.

"And I'm Kat."

She stood up, turned to Rosie. "What a little sweetheart."

"Little terror too," said Fred, laughing. Then he turned to his wife. "I better get back to work. See you at the cottage."

"Don't be too late," said Rosie.

"I'll try not to," said Fred, picking up Agnes and giving her a twirl before handing her back to her mum.

Kat watched the mother and daughter head off, away from the house towards the distant woods, then turned back to Fred.

"They got far to go?" she said.

"Oh, no more 'n half a mile," said Fred. "We live in the old gamekeeper's cottage over the hill there."

Then he turned, his face more serious. "Let's chat, shall we?"

And he motioned them both towards the office.

"HELP YOURSELF to milk and sugar," said Fred Nailor, handing Kat a battered old tin mug, then gesturing towards two chairs that faced his desk. He sat down behind it.

Kat took a seat and looked around the office while she waited for Harry to join her.

Walls lined with bookshelves and framed prints, a small stove in one corner, filing chests, stacks of papers in trays.

On the desk a photo of Fred and his wife, with a baby Agnes in her arms.

Although practical, the office had a softer character than she'd expected. Nailor himself sat patiently, waiting as Harry stirred his regular three teaspoons of sugar into his tea.

"So," said Nailor, looking at Harry, then at her. "You're trying to find out just how Syd died, hmm? That it?"

Kat decided to kick things off.

"His mother can't believe he could have fallen on his gun," she said. "Seems he was fastidious about gun safety, well-trained and all that."

She saw Nailor nod, then shrug. "Of course. I can understand that. These kinds of accidents, they always seem so… I don't know… impossible? That the word?"

Kat nodded.

"But you know – this isn't the first fatal accident I've had to deal with. And I'm sure it won't be the last. And nearly all the incidents I hear about – involve someone who was regarded as a completely safe pair of hands around a weapon."

"Familiarity breeds contempt…" said Harry. "People get careless, you saying? Seen it myself…"

"Exactly," said Nailor. "I also look at it another way – those people with a reputation probably have one because they're handling guns all day, every day."

"Ah – so it's just a matter of time? So many chances to make a mistake?" said Kat.

"Right. It's the odds, you know?" said Nailor. "Spend thousands of hours with a gun in your hands – it only takes a second to make a mistake. A fatal one."

Kat looked at Harry. Nailor's logic was convincing.

"I gather you found the body?" said Harry.

"I did."

"Never easy," said Harry.

"No."

"But – you say you've seen such accidents before," said Harry. "Can I ask you – was there anything about this that seemed different? Looked different?"

Kat saw Nailor think about this carefully. He shook his head.

"What about the wound itself?" said Kat.

She saw Nailor look confused for a second, perhaps uncertain how to explain.

Maybe concerned about a lady being present.

Kat hurried to speak. "Mr Nailor – I spent a year in a nursing station in Amiens, back in '18."

"Ah, right, yes, sorry. Seen it all, hmm? Okay, right – so this was point-blank range, no doubt about it."

"Other injuries?"

"Bad scrape to the poor lad's face – and there was blood on the ground where he'd fallen, so I expect he hit a rock when he landed."

"And nothing to raise any suspicion that it was anything other than a tragic accident?"

"Nothing at all."

Kat paused and looked at Harry. *Time for him to change tack.*

"DID YOU know Syd?" said Harry, picking up his cue from Kat.

"*Know* him?" said Nailor, sounding surprised at the question. "I certainly knew *of* him. Doubt there's an estate manager or gamekeeper on the Downs doesn't know of Syd Buckman. And his father too."

"I imagine there'll be plenty of people happy to see the back of him?"

"Maybe… A bit unfair, that, Harry," said Nailor. "No one wants a young lad cut down like that. But there won't be many tears shed, that's for sure."

"Did you know he was poaching from this estate?"

"Well, I knew *somebody* was. This summer we've lost ten deer already."

"That's a lot."

"Certainly is."

"More than usual?"

Nailor paused. "Many more. Only lost two deer the whole of the rest of the year. Then ten."

Harry picked up on the timing. *Syd behaving strangely, plenty of cash around, the deer poaching out of control…*

He was sure it all connected. *But how?*

"Okay – so this was a recent development? Something new – just in the last couple of months?"

"Was indeed," said Nailor. "And guess who's been getting the blame, hmm? Yes – yours truly."

"Mr Shreeve – he was angry with you, was he?"

"You're telling me. And not just me. Read the riot act to the whole estate staff he did. Had us all doing longer hours. Extra patrols out in the woods. Hired in some help from Arundel, keeping an eye on the north boundary. Even went out himself some nights."

Now that's interesting, Harry thought, *that Shreeve would go out there himself.*

He gave Kat a look, then continued.

"Tough job," said Harry. "Estate must be what… two thousand acres?"

"Nearer four."

"And on the night Syd died – were you out on patrol?"

"All of us were."

"In those woods?"

"Unfortunately, not. We were north of the house – couple of miles away. Big herds always gather there, ripe for the poaching. Heard the shot though."

"Right time – wrong place?" said Harry.

"Exactly."

"But Mr Nailor," said Kat, "surely the cost of all that extra surveillance was more to Mr Shreeve than the price of a few deer? Can't he afford just to take the loss?"

Harry saw Nailor react angrily for the first time in the interview.

"*Afford* to? It's not about affording to! It's the principle. Poaching is stealing! Brazen theft!"

"I'm sorry," said Kat. "I'm not trying to excuse what happened. Just trying to work out how people felt. And clearly they feel strongly."

"That they do. Very strongly." He paused. "And I should apologise too – raising my voice like that. Inexcusable."

"Please, don't even think about it," said Kat. "I completely understand. Sympathise."

"Truth is," said Nailor, "it's put me under a lot of pressure. Lot of long days – nights too. And Mr Shreeve, well—"

But before he could finish, they all heard a loud shout from outside.

"Nailor! Nailor! What the hell's going on?"

Harry saw Fred shut his eyes for a second, as if to control his natural reaction.

"Sorry about that," he said, getting up from his chair. "I'd better go. That's Mr Shreeve."

And he quickly squeezed past them and went outside.

Harry looked at Kat. No words necessary.

They both got up and followed.

9.

INTO THE WOODS

Outside, Kat saw Nailor disappearing round the front of the house. With Harry at her side, she hurried after him.

Turning the corner, she saw the man she guessed had to be Arthur Shreeve, standing by Harry's bike.

Squat, balding, dressed in tweeds even in this warm afternoon sunshine, he stood, arms folded, waiting while Fred Nailor trotted towards him.

"What the hell is this piece of *junk* doing here?"

At that Kat fired a look at Harry.

Did her husband's eyes just narrow at the word "junk"?

"Sorry, sir," said Fred, "it's just—"

"Deliveries, telegrams… how many damn times have I told you? Whatever or whoever it is – tradesman's entrance, not here in front of my bloody house!"

Kat saw him look across at her and Harry.

"And who the hell are *you?*"

Kat put on her sweetest smile and stepped forward, aware that her overalls and windswept appearance weren't going to help much with this introduction.

"Mr Shreeve?" she said, holding out her hand. "Kat Reilly."

"Who?" said Shreeve, the word hurled into the air like a weapon.

He stared at her hand like it was a wet fish and didn't take it.

Kat carried on smiling, her hand still proffered.

"I am *so* sorry about the motorbike. What were we thinking? Leaving it here, dripping oil on your lovely driveway. Harry?" She turned to Harry who now stood at her side. "We really should be careful where we park, don't you think?"

"You're so right, my dear," said Harry, playing along and stepping forward to the bike, as if to wheel it away. "I'll move it right now."

Kat turned back to Shreeve who stood speechless: "What must you think of us?"

"Sir Harry – I'm sure that's not necessary," said Nailor, interrupting presumably to spare his boss's embarrassment.

"*Sir* Harry...?" said Shreeve.

Kat had to admit – *that* was a great moment. Shreeve stopped dead in his tracks, mid-tirade.

Harry gave Shreeve a little wave: "Two ticks. I'll have this, um, *piece of junk* out of your way, Mr Shreeve."

"W-wait a minute," said Shreeve, and Kat could see him slowly cottoning on. "Sir Harry Mortimer? Lady Mortimer? From Mydworth? God, sorry. I didn't realise. There's no need to... Please, leave your bike there. It's just – we don't usually have visitors arrive by..."

"Motorcycle?" said Kat. "A little unconventional, I know, but such a delightful way to travel on a summer's afternoon."

"Yes, yes – I'm sure," said Shreeve, suddenly all smiles. "But I must apologise, I had no idea you were coming to see me?"

"Actually – they came to see me, sir," said Nailor. "Had some questions about the boy that died. The poacher."

"Questions?" said Shreeve, turning back to Harry, as if Kat now was no longer important.

"We're helping Syd Buckman's parents find out exactly what happened to their son, Mr Shreeve," said Kat. "How he died. Where he died."

"He died in my woods with one of my deer dead next to him," said Shreeve, his voice cold.

Kat saw him look across, towards the house. She turned and followed his gaze – to see the girl in the yellow dress now seated on a bench by the front door, head down in a book.

But easily within earshot.

Her appearance seemed to have a calming effect on the blustery Shreeve.

"We were rather hoping that Mr Nailor here would show us the actual place where he died, Mr Shreeve," said Harry. "With your permission, of course."

Shreeve turned back to Kat. "Helping the parents? I see. Well, I suppose as you've asked – and as it's you, Lady Mortimer, I won't stand in your way. Fact – Nailor, why don't we take the car and we'll all go up there together?"

Kat caught Harry's eye, and gave the merest of nods towards the girl by the house.

Melissa.

This is my chance to talk to her, she thought, hoping he'd see what she was thinking.

"That's awfully kind of you, Mr Shreeve," said Harry. "Just the three of us though, I think. I doubt my wife will be keen on traipsing round the woods – that right Katherine?"

Kat kept the smile from her face. *Nicely put, Harry,* she thought.

Though he knows too well I can traipse with the best of them.

"Oh, absolutely," she said, playing the timid wife. "Beautiful day like this? Can't think of anything more *ghastly*."

Shreeve nodded to the girl by the house: "Excellent. My daughter there, will look after you, I'm sure. Some tea, biscuits perhaps?"

He called over. "Melissa!"

Perfect, Kat thought as she watched the girl look up from her book and stare at her father.

"Hmmph," he said. "Seems it's too much for her to come over and say hello. Afraid you'll have to go to her."

"Don't worry, Mr Shreeve, I was a young girl once. Difficult age?"

"God – is it ever," said Shreeve. "Anyway – Sir Harry, Nailor – soon as we get this out of the way, the sooner we can get back here and I can perhaps offer you a proper refreshment?"

"Sounds wonderful," said Harry.

He turned to Kat, clearly enjoying himself. "You have a nice little chat here, Kat, and, um, I'll see you later. You will be okay, won't you?"

"Oh, I think I'll be fine, Harry. Do be careful in the woods, now."

"Oh, will I ever."

She watched as Harry turned back to Shreeve and Nailor, following behind them towards the line of vehicles parked at the side of the house.

And when they were well away…

She turned, and walked over towards Melissa Shreeve.

Time to find out just what the real deal was between this girl and Syd Buckman.

Harry followed Shreeve and Nailor along the path through the woods. Although it was still a good couple of hours till sunset, the thick mesh of oak and birch branches above let very little light onto the forest floor.

They walked in silence. *Not surprising*, thought Harry, *given the grim reason for the journey.*

After ten minutes, they reached a clearing and Nailor stopped.

"This is where Buckman took down the deer," he said, pointing to a flattened area of undergrowth. "Buried what he didn't want to carry."

Harry caught up with him, stared at the ground, then around the clearing.

"He lay in wait over there somewhere, you think?" he said.

"Bastard," said Shreeve.

Harry caught Nailor's eye – said nothing.

"How far to the road from here?" said Harry.

"Half mile," said Nailor.

Harry nodded, and Nailor led the way, this time with Shreeve following.

"WHAT ARE you reading?" said Kat having walked over, and taken a seat next to Melissa on the bench.

The girl raised the book so Kat could read the title: *To the Lighthouse.*

Then she put it down again, as if the chances of it meaning anything to Kat would be zero.

"Really? Used to be my favourite Virginia Woolf," said Kat, looking out at the meadows and distant trees, but aware that she had Melissa's attention.

"*Used* to be?"

"Then I read *Orlando*. You read it?"

"No, I haven't. Um, I'm not sure my father would approve... a book like that... he can be so old-fashioned."

"I'll lend it to you. It's funny. And – in my opinion – not at all... dangerous. Well, at least, no more dangerous than any other books written by a woman."

Melissa laughed, and Kat turned, smiled at her.

Suddenly liking this young girl and her book.

Melissa was maybe older than she looked. Seventeen perhaps? Pretty – but also a little stocky. Determined looking. *A bit of her father in those eyes?*

"I like dangerous," said Melissa.

"Oh, there you go! So do I."

"That bike..." said the girl, putting down her book.

"You like it?" said Kat.

"I'd love to have a bike like that. Love to ride one, one day."

Kat shrugged. "Well, what are we waiting for?"

"You're joking?" said Melissa, her eyes wide. "Can you ride it?"

"Can I ride it?" said Kat, getting up. "Oh, I can ride it."

She walked over to where Harry had parked the bike, grabbed the two helmets, then turned – to see Melissa walking over, mouth almost hanging open.

She threw one of the helmets to the girl, then climbed onto the bike, flicked the fuel switch, held the clutch – and kicked the engine into glorious, throbbing life.

"Come on," said Kat, twisting the throttle. "Just sit tight, grab hold, and lean when I tell you to."

And she waited while Melissa buttoned the helmet, then climbed up behind her, the yellow dress high on her legs.

"Trust me?" said Kat.

"Utterly."

A LITTLE NIGHT MURDER

"So let's go, kid," said Kat.

She let out the clutch, twisted the throttle and slew the bike round in an arc on the gravel – then headed down the drive towards the setting sun.

"Yessss!" called the girl behind her. "Yessss!"

"YOU LOCAL, Fred?" said Harry as they walked carefully down the narrow, wooded path, ribboned with gnarled tree roots.

"Worcester, born and bred."

"How long you been around here?"

"Seven… eight years," said Fred. "Moved here, met Rosie, married in a year."

"Good man he is, Sir Harry," said Shreeve, from behind Harry. "Reliable – when that family of his isn't taking his mind off his work."

Harry noticed Fred didn't say anything.

Probably used to holding his tongue around his boss.

But before they could talk further, Fred stopped.

"Here we are," he said.

And he pointed to a dense wall of shrubs and vegetation, some twenty yards away from the path. Harry followed him. He could see the ground here was rough, uneven, with a real maze of tree roots.

Easy to miss in the dark, and so easy to trip over, thought Harry.

Nailor sank to his haunches, touched the ground.

"Was about ten in the morning when I found him. Or rather, one of my dogs found him. He was lying face down, facing that way – south – towards the wall which runs along the Arundel road. That's the estate boundary. Where he was heading, I expect."

Harry scanned the area, trying to replay the scene in his mind's eye, the boy running through the wood, deer over his shoulder, gun in hand.

"The deer he took – he had it bound onto a carrying pole," said Fred.

"Where was that?" said Harry.

Fred pointed: "Over there – just a few feet away."

"And the rifle?"

"Under the body. He'd clearly been dead for some hours."

Harry nodded.

"How far is the wall?"

"Um, hundred yards perhaps – not much more," said Fred.

Harry stood and walked back to the path, then looked around the clearing. He could see the path continue through the trees.

"Down there?" he said.

"That's right," said Fred. "We found a gap in the fence, section of stone wall shaped to make an easy way into the estate."

Harry walked slowly over to the spot where the body had been found.

"Seen enough?" said Shreeve.

Harry nodded.

"Good. I suggest we head back, have ourselves a whisky at the house."

Harry watched Shreeve lead the way this time, Fred following, then he, too, headed off down the path.

But just before he left the clearing, he paused again, seeing in his mind's eye Syd running through the woods in the darkness, something not making sense.

Something not right. Not right at all.

With the road almost in sight, why did Syd leave the path, and go into the undergrowth?

If he needed a rest, a breather – he wouldn't have stopped there.

And if he didn't… Then what was he doing? You'd only leave the path…

If you were hiding.

But these woods were empty. The keepers were miles away.

Unless…

There was someone else in the woods that night? Someone Syd tried to hide from…

And if so, who?

10.

A MOTIVE FOR MURDER?

Kat walked back to the bench with Melissa, the wild ride on the motorbike having sealed their friendship.

And, before her father got back, an opportunity to ask some questions.

Melissa turned to her. "Would you care for anything? Tea? Glass of water? I can have something brought out."

Kat smiled. "Oh – thank you. No really but—"

Kat sat down hoping young Melissa would follow suit.

"Wondering if I could ask you a few questions? About the boy who died."

"Syd," said Melissa.

Kat nodded and saw Melissa turn away. She wondered if the "good will" she had built up was suddenly fading.

"My husband Harry and I are asking questions, talking to people." Kat took a breath. "To see if it really *was* an accident."

Melissa kept looking away. And now, conversation started, Kat had no option but to continue.

"I mean, he died on your father's land... guess it *could* have been an accident... but just wondering..."

The girl slowly turned back. The sunny smile that had been on her face after the bike ride was gone. And what was there, and what it meant, Kat couldn't tell.

"You mean," Melissa said slowly, "that since he died poaching, stealing my father's deer, you think—" the girl took a long pause, her green-blue eyes locked right on Kat "—that my father had something to do with it?"

"I—I didn't say that."

And at that Melissa shook her head. "He has men to keep the herd safe, now, doesn't he? But—" another look away "—I'd be lying if I said my father didn't wish Syd any harm. Not after he learned that Syd and I… had been friendly. That's what you really want to know, isn't it?"

"I needed to ask you. We're not accusing—"

Melissa's eyes locked back on Kat. "Aren't you?"

Kat decided to keep asking questions: "Were you very close to him, Melissa?"

"I liked him," said Melissa, looking away. "Nothing serious, mind you. Syd was just… *fun*. But that wasn't good enough for my father."

"I see. And what about your mother? What does she—?"

"Oh, she died. When I was little."

Kat nodded, understanding this young woman a little more, now.

"So your father didn't like you seeing Syd."

"Didn't 'like'? He ordered me to stay away from him. God knows what he might have said to him if they'd ever crossed paths." Melissa nodded. "*That's* my father. But he would never do anything."

More head shakes, as if Melissa was considering the impossible.

When, in the distance, the roar of car. Kat thinking: *they must be driving back from the woods where Syd was found.*

But in moments, Kat saw a different car…

And what a car it was!

"You expecting company?"

KAT WATCHED as a red, open-topped car – sporty, sleek and, from the looks of things, fast – came down the drive, then slowed as it reached the gravel circle in front of the Shreeve house.

Kat turned to just catch Melissa roll her eyes.

"It's Tim. You see… *that's* who my father wants me to marry."

"And no sparks there?"

Melissa's voice grew insistent. "I-I'm not sure. He's years older than me, handsome enough, I suppose. But marry him, and you marry his MG too, that new car of his! *And* his whole family." The girl leaned close to Kat for a whisper… "That family? So stuck up!"

Kat laughed at that.

"Not so bad a car though, I'd say. I mean…"

And the cherry-red MG pulled to a sharp stop in front of the doorway.

The driver with a jaunty cap, popped the door open and strolled to the bottom of the steps, facing the two of them.

"What ho! Afternoon Melissa… and… new friend?"

Melissa nodded. "Kat… I mean Lady Mortimer."

"Aha!" He tipped his cap to them. "Good afternoon, m'lady!"

And Kat guessed that this Tim actually knew who she was.

Area like this? Everyone knows everything.

"Welcome to Mydworth, Lady Mortimer! Living at the Dower House, I hear." Tim looked around as if someone was absent from the party. "And where is your better…?"

A LITTLE NIGHT MURDER

"My *husband* is with Mr Shreeve," said Kat, choosing for the moment not to call him out on his 'better half' comment.

"I'm wondering – just a guess of course –" which Kat knew it absolutely wasn't, "if it's all about that messy business with the Buckman boy?"

All through this, Tim kept a smile on his face.

Did Melissa actually like this obviously wealthy young man with the insolent attitude? Or was she just humouring her father?

Kat had to wonder, even in the year 1929, was *that* decision – who to marry, what to do with one's life – really a young girl's to make, or her wealthy and overbearing father's?

A man who clearly had absolutely no use for Syd Buckman.

"I'd offer you both a ride, but see… the old Midget's a two-seater, don't you know? So, what say you and me, Melissa, tootle off for a bit of an afternoon jaunt?"

And once again, Kat felt as if here was a man – good-looking to be sure – nudging a woman to do what *he* wanted.

To make it easy, Kat spoke. "I'm fine to just wait here, Melissa."

Melissa turned to Tim. "Not sure I want to go out, Tim. Just had the most fantastic time on the back of—"

Tim took a step closer.

"Course you do! Top down. Sun out. It'll be an absolute hoot! Just leave a note for dear old Dad."

Then he looked at Kat.

She felt that this young man didn't like her talking to what he viewed as his girlfriend.

In his mind, maybe his potential wife?

Kat repeated. "Go on. Looks a fun ride, still a gorgeous afternoon."

Then, pointedly, "We'll talk more later, all right?"

And at that, Melissa smiled as she got up and walked down to Tim, who raced around to the other side of the MG, and opened the door.

And Kat thought, as she watched the little red car race away, Melissa had given her a lot to think about… and to talk over with Harry.

THROUGH THE car window, Harry spotted Kat sitting by the porch of the Shreeve home, waving.

Alone. *Did she manage to speak to Shreeve's daughter?* he wondered. Was there anything ominous about her being by herself?

He'd know soon enough.

Shreeve pulled up to the front door, and no sooner had Harry opened his door and slid out, when Shreeve turned.

"Sir Harry – you'll join me for a whisky, in the house?"

Less a question than an assumption.

Kat had come down from the porch. He caught her eyes.

There might be more to learn from Shreeve and Nailor; but most important that he got some time to talk to Kat.

Syd Buckman's accidental shooting was looking more suspicious with each person they spoke to.

"Much as I'd love that, I think Lady Mortimer and I need to get back."

"Oh, just a *quick* one, Sir Harry?" Shreeve's previous anger at the dead Buckman and perhaps Harry and Kat's intrusion, was now replaced with a warm glow of affability, under the promise of a warming whisky.

Nailor had gone to the driver's seat, and started the car up to put it away for the day.

"Fred here can join us as well. And——" finally, as if noticing someone who had materialised out of thin air, Shreeve turned to Kat, "Lady Mortimer, I'm sure we can tempt you with a sherry perhaps. Or a glass of port?"

Kat had meanwhile, and much to Harry's relief, walked over and locked her arm tight around his.

And was it his imagination or did she actually lean into him a bit?

As to Shreeve's offer, he couldn't wait to hear how she responded.

"Port, sherry? Think a whisky would do me just fine. But Harry here is quite right, we *do* have things to attend to."

And knowing that Shreeve had his eyes on her, Kat shot Harry a coy look.

My God, thought Harry, *she is* playing *with the man.*

What fun.

Shreeve – with that final rebuff, his imagination perhaps bubbling away – nodded. "Ahem, right, yes. Next time, then."

"Thank you *so* much," said Kat for the both of them as Shreeve nodded.

She led the way to where she had parked the motorbike and they both put on their helmets.

True to her word, she climbed in front, started the bike first time, and smoothly kicked away the stand. Harry slipped smoothly onto the back and locked his arms tight around her.

"Comfy?" Kat said.

"*Quite.* You know, I might prefer this position to actually driving the thing."

"Do hold tight… hate to hit a bump and have my husband get bounced off."

"Oh yes – that would never do. Quite a scandal in Mydworth that would be."

And in response Harry tightened his circling arms around Kat's waist, just a smidge tighter.

She gave the throttle a test burst.

Harry looked over to Shreeve watching the show.

A nod, accompanied by a smile from Harry, and then Kat actually had the bike do a quick, tight circle in the driveway, gravel flying, a move he wasn't sure he could pull off.

Wherever did she learn how to do this? he wondered.

Then she aimed the bike down the long drive, to the front gate and out, sun low, heading for their still-new home.

11.

A STRANGE DISMISSAL

As they raced up the drive, Harry leaned up to Kat's right side, close to her ear.

"Think it makes sense," he said loudly, over the rumbling roar of the bike, "that we don't start chatting here?"

Kat did a quick glance back.

"Home soon enough, my Harry. Imagine we have a lot of things to share. Let's do it over a whisky neat."

"There you go. I do love," again as loud as he could as Kat twisted the throttle a bit more on the long straight, "your planning abilities."

And then he leaned close, enjoying the sunset ride with his rather amazing "chauffeur".

KAT HAD expected as she pulled up to their home, the Dower House, that Maggie would have been gone for the day.

As to the housekeeper's hours, that was never discussed, so Kat had no real idea. Seemed Maggie could be there magically at the most apt times, whether very early in the morning, or now, sunset looming.

As if she had what the mystics – *all the rage in London* – called "extra-sensory perception". Or did she simply have quick side chats, arranging things with Harry?

Now, as she walked into the house, Maggie stood in the small foyer, handbag held close, looking ready to head home.

"Maggie!" Harry said. "Still here?"

The woman nodded. "Had some things to do, getting the house all ready for the rest of the week. I, um, took the liberty of fixing you two a light supper – wasn't sure when you'd be back. Some nice sliced ham from the butcher, and some cheeses and those figs you like, Sir Harry. Oh, and I also chilled a bottle of that wine you mentioned, put it in the refrigerator. I think I picked the right one."

"The Montrachet 1925 Grand Cru?"

"I believe so, Sir Harry." Maggie laughed. "You know me and my French. Totally lost."

Kat took a step forward, trousers dotted with gritty dust from the road, as was her thin jacket and her white collared shirt.

"Maggie – you're a wonder. Sounds perfect! Can we give you a ride home or—"

The housekeeper, and long-time protector of Harry since he was a boy, shook her head. "No, no, I'm *fine*. It's a wonderful evening. Quick walk into town, will be lovely, but, oh—"

Kat saw the woman's face fall. A change of mood as if she remembered something. She watched Maggie undo the clasp of her handbag with an audible click, open it and withdraw an envelope.

"This was brought here for you."

MAGGIE EXTENDED the envelope, and Kat reached out and took it.

On the front, the words were written in a carefully managed cursive handwriting that would have made the nuns proud back in St Vincent's in the Bronx.

"*Sir Harry and Lady Mortimer.*"

Harry turned to Maggie.

"Who's it from?"

Maggie's face, still in a fallen position, a gentle chew to her lower lip, as if she knew sealed messages – in such envelopes – were never a good thing.

Kat would have to agree.

"Elsie Buckman. Mid-afternoon, it was. Not sure if she expected to see either of you here. Seemed so nervous, she did, fidgety like. I said I'd be sure you got it, and then, well, you never saw someone walk away so fast."

Kat nodded, listening.

"As if someone might see her?"

Maggie nodded.

Kat looked to Harry before sliding a fingernail under an open spot on the envelope flap, and ripping it open.

A single sheet of paper.

"Well, go on," Harry said. "You know I can't *stand* suspense."

Kat shook her head.

"This is so wrong. Listen: '*Dear Sir Harry and Lady Mortimer, I must apologise for asking you to look into my poor Syd's death. I loved my boy but it is quite clear to me now that it was all just a terrible accident. I must ask you to stop asking any more questions about the terrible event. Yours respectfully, E. Buckman.*'"

"Well, well," said Harry. "Looks rather as if we've been dismissed?"

"Harry – I told you what it was like there, Elsie talking, then her husband showing up, and suddenly she stops talking."

"And he was more than eager to see you leave?"

Kat nodded.

Harry took a step and took the single sheet of paper. "You think, maybe he made her write this?"

Kat turned to Maggie, observing this, but not – as of yet – saying anything.

"Maggie, how'd she seem… dropping this off?"

"Like I said, Lady Mortimer. In a hurry, nervous."

"Scared?"

"Perhaps. I mean, a quick pass of the envelope to me, then *whoosh*… she was gone."

Kat nodded. "Maggie, you've lived in Mydworth a long time…"

That at last brought a smile back to the dear woman's face. "Oh, that I have, m'lady. Too long, eh, Sir Harry?"

"Tosh! English towns need *more* people like you, Maggie. Which is my way of saying… don't even *think* of retiring to some little cottage by the sea."

"Ha! Me on a beach! Oh, wouldn't that be a sight."

While Kat enjoyed her husband gently joking with the housekeeper, she had a serious question.

"So, having been here a long time, you have seen Elsie Buckman, her husband Billy? Maybe noticed things?"

At this, Maggie's eyes shifted left, the moment a little uncomfortable.

"Well, I don't generally pay any attention to other people's business, m'lady. Small town – doesn't do to do too much of *that*."

Kat nodded. And rather than press Maggie, she waited.

If the woman had something to share she would.

Finally, Maggie's eyes came back to Kat's.

"Small town, yes," she said. "But you hear things, see things – even when you don't mean to. And, well, that husband of hers?

A LITTLE NIGHT MURDER

He's quite a——" Maggie paused. Whatever word she was thinking of did not fall from her tongue lightly, Kat guessed. "Quite a ne'er-do-well. The family, always so poor; him poaching just like he taught his son, no doubt; and drinking up whatever money they have. Every night, down at The Old Station pub, like clockwork. One of that sort…"

"I see." And now Kat turned to Harry.

Because she had an idea.

"Harry… that note. Elsie didn't write that willingly. I'd bet anything on it."

"Thought you didn't like gambling?"

"I should go back to her. She must know something. Whatever her husband's secret is."

"While the old sod is anchored down at the pub?" said Harry looking away, as if evaluating the plan. "Worth a shot. I mean, at least find out why we have been summarily 'sacked'."

Maggie cleared her throat. "Sir Harry, Lady Mortimer, can I just say, do be careful? That Billy, he drinks a lot. And he has a temper, you know what I mean? I'd hate for——"

As if Harry knew exactly what to do, Kat watched him glide over to her and put an arm around her shoulder.

"Now, Maggie you think I'd *ever* let anything happen to my new bride here? Or even me for that matter!"

At that Maggie laughed.

Good, Kat thought. *Don't want the woman, with all her good will, worrying.*

"All right then," Harry said, "we'll take the car, shall we? Billy at the pub, and we——"

"No," Kat said slowly.

"Hmm?"

"Evening like this, the Buckman's cottage not that far to walk. Can talk on the way."

"And the whisky that was looming?"

"That, and Maggie's dinner. And the Montrachet! All waiting when we get back."

Harry turned and gave Maggie a wink. "Now there's an offer I could barely say no to."

"Thank you, Maggie, for everything, as usual," Kat said. "And sure you don't need—?"

"No. Home in a jiff, I will be."

One last time, as Kat turned to the door, Harry by her side, Maggie said, "And again, you two. Be careful!"

And as Harry answered with a ringing "absolutely" as he opened the door, Kat had to remember…

That if Syd was murdered…

Then Maggie's warning words *were not to be taken lightly.*

12.

SECRETS IN THE HOUSE

Harry walked with Kat down the drive but then – instead of crossing the road and heading towards Market Square – he turned left, to skirt around the centre.

"Shortcut. Used to use it as a boy. Goes right past the cricket pitch and also – farther along – straight to Myer's Hill. Our favourite sledging spot in the winter. It was grand! And it also leads us right to the other end of Briar Lane – and the Buckmans'."

"You as a kid. Somehow hard to imagine."

"Me too. Coming back here, well, it brings up a lot."

And that was true. While Harry mostly loved being back in this part of the world, and especially loved showing Kat an England he grew up in…

There were still those memories. His parents…

And yes, he knew he did a very good job of hiding all that.

But someday, perhaps on a walk like this, he'd talk to Kat about that past.

What happened.

But not right now.

"You know, Kat – I've been thinking about where they found Syd's body."

"Yes? You said it was almost like he was hiding."

"That's right. Thing is – whoever he *was* hiding from – must have been pretty at home in those woods."

"True," said Kat. "Another poacher perhaps? Remember Johnny at the pub said Syd had a fight with some poacher a few weeks back?"

"I'd forgotten that. We should try and track him down. Who else fits the bill, you think? Shreeve?"

"Possible," said Kat. "He was out hunting poachers that night. Though Melissa didn't think that her father could be that angry, so worried about her involvement with Syd, that he'd do something drastic."

"Hard for a daughter to conceive. But a man like that? Self-made, I think is the word? That just doesn't happen without some people in his way getting, well, mowed down."

"True. Also, we shouldn't forget, Fred Nailor *knows* those woods – the whole estate. Remember how angry he got when I said maybe poaching wasn't such a big deal?"

"You're right. And Shreeve was certainly putting him under pressure."

"Then there's Billy Buckman," said Kat. "How does he fit into all this, with whatever he's hiding? Feels like there wasn't much love lost there between father and son."

"An excellent question. And what about Syd's friend Chaz? I bet he's no stranger to those woods over the years. Could he have fallen out with Syd over money… or something else? A girl perhaps? Talking of which – that lad Tim you met? Has he got what it takes to get rid of a love rival?"

"I doubt it," said Kat. "Think he'd fall over in a puff of wind. But when love's at stake, who knows?"

They had turned a corner on a narrow path that finally led to the dusty lane that would take them to the Buckman house, the gibbous moon, now free of trees, hitting them squarely.

The light hitting Kat's face.

"But you know something?" said Harry. "And this *is* important. Did anyone ever tell you that when the moonlight hits your face, *just so*, well, it does have a rather stunning effect."

At that, Kat laughed.

As beautiful as she was, Harry knew she could be – especially when complimented – disarmingly shy.

"I do believe you said a similar thing to me that night in Paris, remember?"

"Oh – do I ever."

And then – the door to the Buckman house came into view ahead, through the overgrown bramble that was the garden, the rickety, tumbled-down fence more eyesore than protection.

Only a gaslight or two on, from the looks of things.

"Well – here we go," Harry said.

He saw Kat take a breath.

Whatever this was, it wouldn't be easy…

ELSIE BUCKMAN pulled the door open a crack, her eyes in the scant light showing that the random knocking on the door was totally unexpected. At first, seeing only Harry, she looked confused.

But then, Harry thought, when those eyes lighted on Kat, they showed something different.

Alarm.

Kat made the introductions.

"Mrs Buckman… Elsie… Sir Harry here."

The woman nodded. Harry saw Kat smile, trying to be as gentle as possible with the woman.

"We got your note. Do you think we could come in? Have a word?"

The woman didn't move. "I—I said… what I said. There's no need for the two of you to do anything. That you should—"

He watched Kat take a step forward, her hand reaching to the mother's hand grasping the edge of the open door.

"Just a few minutes? Promise. There's something we don't understand."

The woman then shot her eyes up to Harry.

Not often she gets a member of the aristocracy popping over at supper time.

And Harry wondered, despite what Maggie had said, could they be sure Billy wasn't lurking somewhere in the house? This whole scene about to turn tawdry and messy?

Anything's possible

But then, with a nod, Elsie Buckman backed away, door opening.

KAT KNEW that Harry expected her to press on with questions, and then their big request.

In some ways, she felt guilty. This woman was obviously bullied by her husband, and now the two of them were asking her to take a risk and trust them.

She waited while the woman peered out into the darkness for a few seconds – as if checking there was nobody out there – then slowly shut the door and turned to face them both.

"Elsie, when I was here your husband got angry with me. Wanting me gone."

The words – Kat could guess – perhaps not unexpected.

"Wanting me and Sir Harry to stop. No doubt about it. And—"

Kat felt for the woman dealing with this. It was bad enough to lose a son, but to have all these questions too.

These suspicions…

"Am I right in thinking your husband made you write this?" she said, taking out the envelope and holding it up.

The sight of the note seemed to deflate Elsie Buckman and Kat saw her shoulders droop.

"He says you're *meddling.* Says we got to let things be. Said if I ever let the two of yous in the house again, he'd…"

"When I was here before, Elsie, your husband acted as though he was hiding something," said Kat.

At her side, she felt Harry take a step closer.

"Do you know what that could be?" he said.

And at that, the woman turned away.

And now, as if to steady herself, she put her hands out to grab the back of the simple wood kitchen chair.

Then nothing. Kat looked at Harry, silently both agreeing they must wait till the woman was ready, and she might turn and talk to them. And when she did…

"I… I don't know *anything.* That Billy, he barely talks to me. But I can tell you this – back in June, it was – I heard him and Syd, talking, loud like. Arguing, back and forth."

"They fought a lot?" Harry said.

The woman nodded. "All the time. But this… I don't know what it was about, but Syd had gone somewhere, then come back next day. Maybe it was about money. Billy… always going on about the money. Maybe not, but—"

The lips began shivering. A gasp of air.

"Somehow I think Billy found out what Syd was doing. But I— I—"

And, at that, Kat saw Harry, so tall for such a cramped, dingy cottage, walk over to the woman as if to steady her.

The gentlest of hands on her arm.

"Mrs Buckman," Kat heard Harry say, his voice barely a whisper, "if we could look in Syd's room? We might just find something there. Something that will tell us what's been going on? Maybe even what happened to Syd. Do you think—"

And Kat heard a snap outside – a twig, or maybe a dead branch tumbling down in a summer's night breeze.

Or Billy.

That would, certainly make things interesting, she thought.

But no one came to the door, while she and Harry waited for an answer.

And the woman pulled away from Harry to look up at him, then Kat.

"Yes, I mean, I haven't been up there at all, since it happened. Couldn't bear it. But yes. Go on, take a look. Help me—" her throat tight, tears in her eyes still glistening "—put my son to rest. Find out... what you can."

And at that, Harry nodded to the woman. A look to Kat.

"We'll be fast," she added, as Harry turned to the small staircase, a simple flight up, where both of them had to duck down to enter the attic-like upstairs.

Up to Syd Buckman's room.

"GOD – WHAT'S that *smell*?" said Kat, putting her hand to her nose.

The door to Syd's closet-sized room pushed open, Harry already inside filling it, and the rank odour... really strong.

"Well, I imagine if you spend your nights shooting game, breaking it down for transport and sale, some of it's going to rub off on you. Literally."

"I'll say. Well – if there's anything in this room, shouldn't be hard to find it. So small."

"I'll spare you the, er, fun, of rummaging in his old clothes... checking pockets and all that."

"What a gentleman I've married. I'll take the dresser, that table... Not looking very hopeful is it?"

"'Fraid not. Still, we may be lucky."

And as Kat squeezed by Harry, past the narrow single bed with dingy sheets that – she guessed – hadn't been changed in a long time, she slid open drawers.

To see - boxes of gun cartridges.

Tools of the trade.

A large serrated knife in its sheath.

Probably Syd has a number of those, she thought.

Then, surprisingly, a photograph.

It took a moment for Kat to recognise the person in the centre: three girls in school uniforms, arms locked around each other.

"Find something?" said Harry.

"That's Melissa, there," said Kat, holding up the snap so Harry could see. "Guess Syd got her to give it to him."

"Thought you said those two were not really boyfriend, girlfriend and all that?"

Kat shook her head. "That's right. I think – a young girl just having fun. Not serious, for her at least. Maybe just rebelling against her dad."

"And that is one powerful dad to rebel against. Yuck."

Kat turned to see Harry holding up a pair of coveralls, dark maroon smears on the material, the blood from a night's poaching she assumed. Then she saw him reach down under the bed…

"Hell-lo – what have we here?"

Harry held up a pair of slightly cleaner trousers – corduroys. He pulled out a fistful of papers from a pocket and spread them out on the bed.

"Okay. Boarding house receipt. The Old Orchard. Oh, here, look a rail ticket. Return to Bristol – dated third of June. Bristol? Hmm. Why go to Bristol?"

Kat reached down and grabbed what looked like a torn piece of a cigarette packet no more than an inch by an inch, folded in half.

Read it.

"*Tom Mulcahey.*"

"Well, that's interesting," Harry said. "I wonder… who is this 'Tom Mulcahey'?"

"Name doesn't mean anything to you?"

"No. Been away though so… Could be a local, I suppose."

"You know," Kat said, "you write a name down like that, very carefully, on the back of a cigarette packet when you *don't* know the person. Not someone you know… but more a name you need to remember."

"Yes. I mean, that's what I do," Harry said. "I wonder – does it have something to do with Syd's going to Bristol?"

"Maybe."

Which is when, from downstairs came the sound of a door slamming open against the interior wall of the house, followed by a bellow, sounding slurred even from up here.

"*Bloody* hell, *woman!*"

"We got company," Kat said.

"Oh, good. I love surprises," said Harry grinning.

But then, that grin fading.

"Not sure now's the best time for you to introduce me to the delightful Billy Buckman," he said. And she saw him turn to look at the small window over the bed.

"You thinking what I'm thinking?" she said.

"Can't be more than a ten-foot drop. And don't forget – I've already seen you escape through a bedroom window before."

She climbed onto the bed and pushed open the window as quietly as she could, looked out.

Easy, she thought.

"What are we waiting for?" she said. And she climbed through, twisted round, then dropped to the ground.

Looking up, she saw Harry emerge, pulling the window shut behind him as he half-hung, half-crouched on the sill. Then he swung loose and dropped, got to his feet, rubbing his hands, and gave her a wink.

They stood together in the shadows watching and listening.

Listening. To see if Billy started on his wife.

But all was quiet now in the house.

"Think he must have just conked out," Harry said.

"Hope so. Poor old Elsie won't know what happened to us." And then, as they slipped past the bramble, to the broken gate out to the lane, Kat said, already figuring out a plan: "Tomorrow morning? Early? To Bristol?"

"Have to. That train ticket – it's the only lead we've got to Syd's mystery trip. Hope the weather holds."

Onto the lane, Kat locking arms with him.

"So – tell me, Sir Harry – just how far away is this Bristol?"

And, at that, Harry laughed.

"I keep forgetting. You know absolutely *nothing* about my homeland. Not too far at all. Few hours."

"I think tomorrow," Kat announced, "is going to be one – um – very interesting day."

"That it will be."

"But first – ham, cheese and figs."

"And that chilled Montrachet. How did I ever live without a refrigerator?"

"Just wait till the washing machine arrives."

"We'll be the talk of the town, Kat Reilly."

"I think we already are," said Kat.

13.

WHITE LIES

Harry parked the Alvis just down the street from the Old Orchard pub and turned the engine off. He turned to Kat.

"Quite a drive."

"Tell me about it. That was one big herd of cows we had to wait for! Next time, maybe we'll go by train?"

Harry eased open the car door and stepped out, stretched his aching back.

Even though they'd started at first light, the trip from Mydworth to Bristol had taken nearly four hours. They'd shared the driving and stopped a couple of times for a breather – but still he felt exhausted. He watched as Kat climbed out, stretched her back too, then took in the area.

The Old Orchard pub had been easy enough to find – right in the middle of the docks area on Spike Island, set in a warren of tiny terraced houses.

No cars parked in the streets here – though there was a continuous bustle of vans, trollies, weary horses and rickety carts all around.

He looked over at the pub. The shutters were closed and the place seemed deserted. He looked at his watch.

"Should be open soon," he said. "How do you think we should play it?"

"By ear, I guess," said Kat, grinning. "First time to Bristol, you see."

And just then, the door of the pub swung open and a grim-faced woman appeared, dressed in a floral apron, her hair tied back with a twist of cloth. In one hand she carried a pail of water and a brush: Harry watched as she knelt down and set to cleaning the doorsteps.

"Got an idea," said Kat. Before he could say anything, she picked up his briefcase from behind the seats and strode across the road towards the pub.

"WE'RE NOT open," the woman barked, without even looking up from her work as Kat approached.

"I know," said Kat.

The woman stopped brushing, turned and peered up at Kat, her face suspicious.

"Then – what do you want?"

"Wondered if we might have a chat?" said Kat.

"Whatever you're selling – we don't need it."

"Not selling," said Kat. "Fact – I'm buying."

"Like I said – you got ears, *'aven't yer?* – we're <u>shut</u>."

"Not buying a drink – though I sure could do with one. Buying five minutes of your time."

At this, the woman dropped her brush in the bucket, wiped her hands on her apron and stood up. Kat waited while she inspected her for a few seconds, and looked across the road at the roadster, where Harry leaned against the hood.

She saw him doff his hat politely at the visual interrogation.

"Five minutes," said the woman, and she disappeared inside the pub.

Kat turned to Harry and held up her hand – mouthed "five minutes" – and followed the woman.

"LET'S HEAR what you have to say then," said the woman, as Kat joined her at a scratched and weathered old table in the corner of the pub.

With the shutters still closed there was barely light enough to see. Growing up, Kat had worked a New York bar not so different from this and she knew the sights and the smells intimately.

The chairs upended on tables, the smell of strong bleach mixing with the fug of last night's tobacco smoke, spilt beer, whisky, sweat, cheap perfume.

She pulled up a stool, sat, put a pound note on the table.

"One now. One if you tell me what I need."

She watched the woman take the note, fold it, tuck it into the top of her blouse.

"Go on."

"How long have you worked here?"

"Ten year."

"Were you working here in June?"

"Might have been."

"Yes or no?"

"Yes," said the woman, with a shrug.

"Good. Now – you have rooms, yes?"

"We do."

Kat lifted the briefcase, took out the receipt and laid it on the table.

"You recognise it?"

She watched as the woman picked up the receipt, read it, put it down.

This is like pulling teeth, she thought.

"I wrote it," said the woman. "So what?"

"The man you gave it to – Syd Buckman. You remember him?"

"We got four rooms, missy. Summer they're all taken. Different bloody sailor every night. How should I remember one bloke from way back in June? And more to the point – why? Not in trouble, is he?"

Kat sat back. Time to get… *creative.*

"On the contrary. I'm here representing, a client from New York who was staying in Bristol that month. A very wealthy person who must remain anonymous. She had a bad fall. A kind young man looked after her in the street, put his jacket around her, helped her to hospital. My client never saw him again. She now wishes to reward this young man. And the only clue we have to his identity – is this receipt found in his pocket, identifying him as Syd Buckman. I have travelled from New York to find him. I *must* find him."

She took another pound note from her purse, placed it on the table, but kept her hand firmly on top of it. She saw the woman look at the note, then back at her.

Would she fall for the story?

"All right. Now I come to think about it – I do remember him. Young lad, yes?"

"That's right."

"Stayed just the one night."

"You sure it was him?"

"Wasn't a sailor, was he? Country lad. Stood out a mile."

"You talked to him?"

"He talked to me, *more* like. Bit of a charmer – least he thought he was."

"He say where he lived?"

"He didn't give much away. From the accent, Sussex maybe? Dunno."

Kat took out her notebook, started scribbling. Something she'd learned over the years, first in New York, then on government service: *the notebook focuses the witness's mind.*

"That's very helpful, thank you," said Kat. Then casually: "I don't suppose he said why he was here in Bristol? Do you think maybe he was taking a boat somewhere? If so, I've probably missed him."

"Oh, I don't think he was off on some journey."

"Really?"

"Morning he left, he had his breakfast then he asked me how to get to the library."

Kat had to hide her surprise. "The *library*? You mean – a local library?"

"No – the big one. College Green."

"You're sure?"

"Course I'm sure." The woman laughed. "Not a question I get every day! And he didn't look like the bookish type – that's how I remember."

"Appearances deceive," said Kat, really to herself.

"Don't they, though?" said the woman. She looked at a big clock on the far wall. "Five minutes."

Kat slid the note across the table – and the woman slipped it into her hiding place.

"One last question."

"Go on," said the woman, then she laughed. "You can have this one on me!"

"There was another boy who we think helped that day – Tom Mulcahey. Name mean anything?"

110

The woman shook her head. "No. Mulcahey? Nothing." As she stood up, she gave Kat a thin smile: "Seems like there was a lot of *helpful* young men out on the streets of Bristol that day. Your... boss... she sure *was* lucky, wasn't she?"

"Very," said Kat, holding the woman's eye, then taking up her briefcase and heading to the door.

Out on the step, she turned. "Thanks for your help."

The woman stood in the doorway, arms folded.

"Any time," she said, nodding over Kat's shoulder to where Harry stood, hat in hand, still waiting. "By the way – who's he?"

Kat turned to look at Harry, then back at the woman.

"Him? Oh, he's my driver."

"Quite the looker."

"Isn't he? Came with the car."

"He spoken for?" said the woman.

"I believe so," said Kat.

"Shame," said the woman. Then she nodded, and crouched down again to her pail and brush.

Kat turned and walked across the street, past a lumbering horse and cart, to the car.

"Bristol library please, driver," she said, climbing into the front seat and keeping a straight face.

"Certainly, madam," said Harry, giving her a smart salute, then starting up the engine and driving them both away.

HARRY WALKED with Kat across the grand entrance hall of Bristol Library, their footsteps echoing on the shining marble floor.

"A looker?" said Harry.

"That's what she said."

A LITTLE NIGHT MURDER

"I like that. The woman clearly has sound judgement, as well as taste."

"Don't you think it's more important what I discovered about Syd?"

"Of *course*," said Harry. "But I wouldn't have expected anything less from you."

Ahead, Harry could see the reception desk for the reference library, and in front of it a short queue. A woman sat behind trays of paperwork and index cards, dealing with visitors to the library.

Harry looked at Kat – who nodded at him – as if to say, "now it's your turn".

"Any idea how to play this one?" she said. "Doing a lot of improvising today."

"Oh. None whatsoever. Just going to have to trust those wonderful instincts."

He smiled at Kat, then turned and watched the process under way ahead.

Thinking....

They knew that Syd had probably come here back in June. But they were only *guessing* he visited the reference library, and it seemed unlikely anyone here would remember his visit.

But then, at the very last minute, as he watched the man in front fill out a form and move on into the library, a plan began to form.

"Yes?" said the woman, barely looking up as he stepped forward.

"Good day," he said, giving her his most charming smile. "I was here back in June, doing some research, you know, and I need to show my colleague here the material. She's over from New York – only here in Bristol for the day."

The woman looked up, clearly assessing Kat's suitability. "Madam will need to fill out a form."

"Excellent," said Harry, and he watched Kat step forward and take pen and form.

"I'm sure it's an awful bother too, you know," said Harry, "but for the life of me I can't remember which volumes I was working on when I was here. I wonder – would you mind awfully grabbing the old search cards for me, checking? Would save so much time…"

"Hmm," said the woman. "We don't normally—"

"I really would appreciate it," said Kat, handing her form over. "It's really my only chance, and the facilities here look *so* much better than New York."

Deft use of an American accent, with perfect timing, Harry thought.

"Well, just this once," said the woman. Then she turned to Harry. "Name?"

"Buckman," said Harry, smiling. "Sydney Buckman."

14.

TRUTH REVEALED

Kat sat at an empty desk next to Harry in the main Reading Room of the library. Dotted around them at other tables in the dusty afternoon light sat other researchers – students, academics perhaps – huddled over notebooks amid stacks of books.

So far, the mysterious "volumes" that Syd Buckman had ordered back in June hadn't emerged from the stacks.

She saw Harry check his watch.

"Lunchtime already," he said. "Whatever is—"

"Shhhhh!" came a voice from behind one of the piles of books.

Kat smiled at Harry and was about to whisper to him when she spotted two library assistants heading their way, their arms filled with enormous leather-bound books.

"Mr Buckman?" said one, stopping at their desk.

Harry nodded. The two assistants laid the great volumes carefully, almost reverentially, on their table, then turned and went without a further word.

Kat looked at Harry, then dragged one of the volumes over and read the inscription on the spine:

"*Bristol Evening Press*, 1920, January 1st to 31st March. What—?"

"Four volumes, covering the whole year?" said Harry, shaking his head and pulling one of the books towards him. "Bound copies of the local newspaper. And I wonder what the hell's so special about 1920?"

Together they slowly lifted the heavy, leather cover of volume one to reveal the original newspapers, great broadsheets filled with dense newsprint, carefully bound.

"Three hundred and sixty-five editions," he whispered. "'Fraid this might take a while."

"Three hundred and sixty-*six*, actually," said Kat. "And no index. What in the world are we looking for?"

"I have absolutely no idea," said Harry with a shrug. "But at a guess, anything to do with Mydworth, and perhaps poaching?"

"Add Shreeve?"

"Maybe. Good idea. And don't forget our 'mystery man', Mr Mulcahey."

Then she watched Harry as he stood up, removed his jacket, placed it on his chair, sat down, dragged a volume close.

"Reminds me of school exams," he said. "And not in a very nice way, mind you."

"Your time starts now," said Kat, and she, too, bent forward to start reading.

TWO HOURS later, Harry stood up to close the binder on the first of his two volumes. His eyes were swimming with the strain of scanning so many articles, the print so tiny, the concentration intense.

He looked over at Kat as she, too, finished her volume and wearily slid the great book away.

"Nothing?" she said.

"*Rien!* Though I did catch up on some of the cricket scores I missed that year. Awful Test series. Glad I missed it. Think I was in Athens."

He checked his watch and frowned – just two hours until the library closed.

Together they reached for their second volumes, both hands required to open the heavy covers.

"This is like looking for a needle in a haystack, without even knowing you're looking for a needle," he whispered, leaning closer to look at the first page.

But Kat didn't answer. He glanced across – and from her face could tell instantly she'd found what they were looking for.

"Kat?"

She nodded – her face looking drawn, shocked.

He slid his chair across, put one hand on her arm to comfort, looked down to the newspaper where her finger now pointed.

There, on the first page of the first newspaper, in amongst the dense print and the tiny adverts for local businesses – he saw one small photograph, a headline, and an article.

The headline – *Murder Suspect Escapes in Court Debacle.*

The photograph – *a face so familiar, albeit ten years younger.*

The story – *Local man, Tom Mulcahey, 25, accused of the brutal murder of fellow dock-worker and father of two, Sam O'Leary, in a public brawl in March, fled court yesterday and is now believed to be on the run…*

Harry read the short article, looked at the photograph again, then turned to look at Kat, hardly believing it could be true. But there was no doubt.

Tom Mulcahey, wanted for murder…

Was in fact *Fred Nailor,* estate manager on the Shreeve Estate, Mydworth.

"It's him, isn't it?" he said.

"I can't really believe it," said Kat, her voice barely a whisper. "Nailor seems such… such a gentle man."

"He must have got away, taken a new identity. Started a new life in Sussex."

"But what does it mean? You think this is what Syd was looking for – what he found?"

"Can't be a coincidence, can it? Question is, what did Syd do with the information?"

Suddenly the musty research room felt chilled.

"You think it got him killed?"

Harry shrugged, still trying to piece together what might have happened.

"All I can think of is Nailor's poor wife – and that sweet little girl – oh God, Harry."

She turned to face him, and Harry saw such sadness in her face. He thought of the dreadful ripple of events that would now follow their discovery, a ripple that would turn into a great wave, *smashing into so many lives.*

She stared at him for a few seconds, then he saw her take a deep breath.

"We need to make notes," she said. "Get all the facts down. Then head home. Okay?"

He saw her reach for a pen and pull her notebook close. Seeing how she seemed instinctively to be able to channel her feelings into action.

And as she wrote, he pondered on the next task – trying to figure out how this discovery had led to Syd Buckman's death.

And soon he had a plan how to do just that.

IT WAS STILL light by the time they got back to Mydworth, and Kat watched the locals chatting on sidewalks, or sitting outside the pubs laughing, joking together, as Harry threaded the big car carefully through the streets of the town towards Briar Lane.

Her stomach had churned the whole way – but she knew it was not with hunger: they'd picked up a late lunch of bread and cheese and filled a flask of water in Salisbury and eaten while they drove.

No, not hunger. But a feeling of deep sadness – and dread for what lay in store for Fred Nailor's family.

As the miles had rolled by, they had talked through exactly what they had to do now to bring the man to justice.

For whatever crime – or crimes – he had committed. And how best they might protect the innocents in this desperate situation.

The two of them had sat in silence until Harry pulled up in the narrow lane outside the Buckman's cottage.

Together they climbed out, and walked up to the front door. From the sound of arguing deep within, Kat knew that Billy Buckman was home.

Good – because he was why they were here.

Harry knocked on the door, sharply. The arguing stopped – and seconds later the door swung open. She saw Billy standing there, filling the door frame, face flushed, eyes burning. "You lot. I told *you*," Billy levelled a finger at Kat, "that we was *done* with your silly questions, and as this is my damn house, I want—"

Kat watched as Billy didn't get to finish that demand.

Harry stepped forward and – as if snatching a bug from the air – he reached up and gave the finger and the hand it was attached to (and the arm) a twist.

Billy's immediate response was a *yelp*, and – besides trying to squirm to avoid the painful twist – he also caved forward as if to fall to his knees on the doorstep.

All in one smooth move.

Whatever did they teach my husband in the diplomatic corps? thought Kat.

That is one neat trick.

"Sorry, old boy," Harry said, releasing the finger, but not until it had done its work. "Don't think I mentioned my wife here just doesn't like people pointing their fingers at her. Isn't that right, dear?" Harry said turning towards Kat.

"Absolutely loathe it," she said.

"There you *go*," Harry said; wheeling back to Billy who was still in a crumpled state, though the source of his contortions had passed.

"Must be an American thing. Who knows! Anyway, Mr Buckman – Billy – why don't we step inside to continue this little chat? Awfully rude to leave us on the doorstep, don't you think?"

And here, Harry shifted his demeanour and stepped past Billy and into the tattered cottage.

It was amazing to Kat how one second he could be funny and light – and the next he could turn so fierce… *when it was needed.*

I like that about him, she thought.

Inside, Kat saw Elsie Buckman pressed tight into a corner, hands wringing a cloth, eyes rabbit-like, as her husband staggered back into the cottage clutching his arm.

"So, let's start this all over again," said Harry. "You were up to something with your son, Syd. In fact, I'm guessing you well knew about his little visit to Bristol."

Harry waved the boarding house receipt in front of the man.

"You knew what Syd was doing – didn't you Mr Buckman?" said Kat. She paused, aware that the dead boy's mother stood near. But there was no other way to phrase it. "What might have gotten your son killed?"

For a moment it seemed to Kat that Billy – in his near comical Quasimodo stance – was speechless. His gummy mouth did open once or twice, gulping at the air like a fish out of water.

"We've spent the day in Bristol, Billy. And I imagine, with all that we now know, Sergeant Timms is going to want a little chat with you." Harry added.

And as if they were playing a dizzying game of tennis doubles, Kat added, "Or you could tell us all. Help us. Help your wife. And maybe you won't go down for as long."

And slowly Billy righted himself.

Sniffed at the air, eyes darting left and right as if there might be an exit somewhere that he didn't know about.

Or maybe simply trying to regain some of his dignity.

Not much of that on display here, she knew.

"All right. I tell *yers.* No need for the police."

The man fired a look at his wife.

That look – maybe signalling that whatever Billy was about to say – would be painful.

"I taught the boy all I knew. But this thing he got into… He didn't get it *all* from me."

BILLY, AS HE talked, had walked to the kitchen cabinet with its half bottle of cheap whisky.

But Harry gave him a look, a shake of the head.

Best we try to keep his thoughts as clear as possible.

Billy's hand, in mid-arc to take the bottle down, obeyed the silent command.

And Harry, for one, couldn't wait to hear what he was going to say.

"When Syd came back, and started splashing money around, I knew somethin' was up. Found out it was Bristol he went to, and, well, told him that he damn well *better* share what he was up to *with* his old man. *We* supported him all those years, y'know."

Harry kept stock still. Were they about to find out how Syd came to be killed?

"So, he told me. Started down the King's Arms, it did. A poacher fella. Tipped Syd off that someone in town wasn't who they said they were, that they had done bad things in Bristol. And for a bright bloke, who didn't mind takin' a chance… might be an opportunity."

"Blackmail?" Harry said.

Billy nodded.

"And you knew who this was? Who your son was blackmailing?" Kat said.

Harry noted Kat's clipped tone. *She certainly knew how to ask the difficult questions.*

"No. See, that's why he had to go to Bristol. Had a name."

"Tom Mulcahey?"

"Eh? Yeah, *that's* the one. Mulcahey. Anyways, Syd knew who this Mulcahey was pretending to be – but he didn't know *what* this person had done. But, see, he found out all that, he did, right up there. In Bristol."

Harry looked at Kat. Took a breath.

Big question.

"And did he tell you who it was?"

But, at that, Billy shook his head.

"Nah. Wouldn't tell me that. No matter how much I yelled at the stupid boy! But he said, okay, if I stayed quiet, I could have some cash. And with me bein' his dad and all, I did as he asked."

"That. And for the money," Harry added.

What a loving father.

"Seemed only fair, expenses in the house, bed and board… so, yes."

"Just to be clear, Billy. Syd took the name to Bristol. Learned what this person had done. So – besides his poaching – he then added blackmail to his activities? And you knew? Helped him?"

Billy had the eyes of a caged animal, Harry saw.

Lick of the lips as he finally nodded.

Now Harry took a step towards the man. *Did he ever think to warn his son away from such a dangerous game?*

Not Billy Buckman.

"Is there anything else we need to know?"

"N-not that I know, Sir Harry. I *swear* it."

Harry nodded and turned to Kat. And Kat had turned to Elsie Buckman, who he guessed had to be scared for so many reasons.

What would happen next?

Kat already talking to her – low voice. "Elsie, I want you to stay in touch with Nicola. She's moving the Women's Voluntary Service office. But it will still be in Mydworth, to help, if you need anything."

And, at that, Harry saw Kat shoot one nicely menacing glance at Billy.

"*Anything* at all. And you know where Sir Harry and I live?"

The woman nodded.

"All right, Kat. I think we're done here," said Harry.

He started for the door, opening it, the night air with a slight chill, but still a gentle late summer's eve.

And once outside, Kat stopped. *Listening.* To see if Billy had started on his wife again.

Silence.

"I think he will watch himself," Harry said to her, guessing the reason for stopping.

"He'd better."

And they climbed back in the car. Before Harry started the engine, Kat turned to him.

"I'm guessing the next step is to bring in the police?"

"Has to be," said Harry. "We don't know if Nailor killed Syd Buckman. But we do know he's on the run from another killing. And he must stand trial for that."

Kat nodded. "It's late though, isn't it?"

"You thinking it can wait until morning?"

"I'm thinking it *should* wait until morning," said Kat. "That family – we can't break them up, not tonight. Now… at this hour? That would be heartless. Whatever Nailor has or hasn't done, I don't want to make it worse for more innocent victims,"

Harry nodded. "You're right. He's going nowhere. Let them have one last night together."

He started the car, and as he pulled away, he felt Kat slide across the seat and lean into him, her head on his shoulder.

And she stayed like that all the way home.

15.

JUSTICE

Kat stood with Harry by the Alvis in the early morning sunlight, watching as two of Timms' constables led Fred Nailor – hands cuffed together in front of him – from the estate office, and loaded him in the back of the police truck.

Before the double doors closed on him, Nailor briefly looked over at her and Harry.

"You know," Nailor said suddenly. "I w—was just trying to protect my family. I couldn't let anything happen to them, now, could I?"

As he spoke, Kat realised something.

This was his defence.

As Timms' constables slammed the doors shut on him, she reflected that sometimes people get pushed into desperate corners.

Maybe – most times – that's the way it is with murder, she thought.

A movement at Shreeve's house caught her eye. She turned.

In one of the front bedrooms she could see Melissa standing, staring out. But this time the girl didn't step back into the shadows.

As the truck drew away down the gravel drive, Kat now saw Shreeve himself emerge from the estate office and walk towards them.

"Bad business," he said, shaking both their hands. "Bad business altogether."

Kat nodded.

"Damned inconvenient too," said Shreeve. "Good managers aren't two-a-penny, you know. He'll be hard to replace."

"I hope that means Mr Nailor's wife and daughter will be safe in their cottage, at least for a short while," said Kat.

"Cottage goes with the job," said Shreeve. "They'll have it for as long as it takes me to find a new hire."

Kat sensed Harry's eyes on her – perhaps hinting now was not the time to fight this fight.

He's right, thought Kat. *But I'll just drop a hint…*

"Of course," she said "But Nailor hasn't yet been tried for the Bristol death. And there's no proof he had anything to do with Syd Buckman's accident."

"Oh, he'll swing for one of them. Both if I had my way," said Shreeve. "You mark my words. It's clear Nailor was a wrong'un, and the tragedy is he took us all for fools for so long. I'm just damned grateful the two of you saw through his little game."

"Mr Shreeve," said Kat, "I really don't think…"

"Ah well," said Harry, and Kat saw him step closer to Shreeve. "Mustn't get ahead of ourselves, must we, Mr Shreeve? Now, I wonder, Lady Mortimer here is inclined to be the one to go down to the Nailors' cottage – do the explaining."

"Is she indeed?" said Shreeve, turning to Kat. "Have at it then, Lady Mortimer. Rather you than me, my dear."

Kat didn't smile, and Shreeve, looking uncomfortable, returned his gaze to Harry.

"So, I was thinking," continued Harry, "that perhaps now might be an opportunity for you and I to have that whisky you offered me the last time we were here?"

"Whisky? Hmm, trifle early but, hell – morning like this, police and all that – why not? Could do with your advice on how to find a replacement for Nailor, Sir Harry. Don't want to hire another bad apple, do I?"

Kat saw Harry nod at her, then she watched him turn with Shreeve and head back towards the house. As they did, she saw Melissa emerge from the front door and walk past her father, with a barely acknowledged wave of one hand, towards the car.

"Lady Mortimer," she said.

"Kat, please. How are you?"

Melissa shrugged, then nodded towards the group of police cars that had remained, parked by the estate office.

"What are they doing, do you think?" said the girl.

"Looking for clues, I imagine," said Kat. "Evidence."

"Isn't it horrible? All this, I mean. My father says you and Sir Harry found it all out."

Kat nodded. Then she had a thought.

"Melissa – how well do you know Mrs Nailor – and her little girl?"

"Very well," said Melissa. "Little Aggie's so much fun."

"I wonder. I'm going to go to the cottage now, to tell Mrs Nailor what's happened. It's going to be a shock – a terrible shock – I'm sure. And I wonder if—"

Kat didn't need to finish.

"Would you like me to take care of Agnes? Stay close to her? You're going to need that. Of course. When shall we go? Now?"

"Now would be perfect," said Kat.

And with Melissa at her side, she turned and headed across the gravel towards the woods where she knew the Nailors' little cottage lay.

If the worst happened, and Nailor was found guilty, someone was going to need to support this woman and her daughter.

And she had an instinct that Melissa was going to be key to that.

"CHEERS," SAID Harry, raising his whisky and soda and clinking glasses with Kat.

"Chin-chin," she said. He watched as she took a sip of her gin and tonic, then sat back in the big leather Chesterfield, the early evening light streaming through mullioned windows. "God – I needed that."

The bar of The Eagle and Child – Mydworth's oldest hotel, all oak beams and big sofas – was empty, and though Harry could see the barman cleaning glasses, he doubted they would be overheard.

"Quite a day, hmm?" he said.

"Tell me about it," said Kat. "Good idea coming here for dinner. Think we deserve a treat."

"Absolutely."

"Any news from Timms?"

"Nailor's admitted to his true identity. Seemed almost relieved to be found, apparently."

"I can understand that. I guess he turned over a new leaf here, but that past must have been a burden. What's he saying about Syd Buckman?"

"Not much. He's confirmed the lad was blackmailing him. Forcing him to let Syd take deer too."

"But not that he killed him?"

"No," said Harry, shaking his head. "And if they can't prove he was in those woods, they don't have a case."

"You think he was?"

"I do," said Harry. "One of Shreeve's men – a young lad – saw him slip away from the group that night."

"And didn't mention it at the time?"

"Being loyal, I suppose," said Harry. "When Timms told him about Nailor's past, he said what he'd seen. Whether Nailor meant to kill Syd – or it was just a fight that boiled over – I don't know. But, by all accounts, the Bristol case will take him down anyway."

"So Shreeve was right. He'll pay with his life."

Harry nodded. "Most likely. Must have been tough this morning – Nailor's wife? The little girl?"

"Couldn't have done it without Melissa," she said.

"I like her," said Harry. "A lot more than I like her father, I have to confess!"

"I think she's with you on that. By the way – I mentioned her to Nicola at the WVS? I think she could be a useful volunteer."

"Good idea. You saw her today then?"

"Dropped in this afternoon, just to bring her up to date with things."

"Good," said Harry. "None of this would have happened if it hadn't been for Nicola's persistence… and wanting to help."

He looked at Kat – sitting forward, her brow slightly wrinkled – sensing she had something important to say. "She say anything interesting?"

"Ha, you know me too well, Harry," said Kat, taking a sip of her gin, putting it down on the table and leaning closer. "She *did* actually. She's found a new office, right in the centre of town, bit more space… and guess what? She has enough money to run it properly for another year. Anonymous benefactor apparently."

"Good for her."

"Totally. But what it means is – well – she asked if I could help out. At the WVS. Couple of days a week, you know? What do you think?"

"I hope you said yes!"

"I did. Start Monday."

"Well, good for you," said Harry, raising his glass to her. "It's a terrific cause and you know that you'll be wonderful."

"Just paperwork, of course, to start with," said Kat. "Talking to women who come in. Taking notes. Nothing like… well… like this *case*."

"Good Lord, no," said Harry.

"I mean – Mydworth's a quiet little town really, isn't it? It's sure to be just marital issues, employment problems, difficult children…"

"Bound to be," said Harry.

"Not that I don't like the excitement."

"Of course."

"Or miss using some of those… *skills*… I appear to have acquired in the service of my country."

"Absolutely."

"Or facing up to unknown dangers with you."

"Totally."

"So – here's to the quiet life, husband mine," she said, raising her glass to his again.

But before Harry could clink glasses, the hotel concierge came over, bent low to the table.

"Sir Harry Mortimer?"

"That's me."

"Telephone call for you, sir, in the manager's office. And, um, they said it was urgent."

Harry turned to Kat and raised his brows. She raised hers back.

Then he stood, picked up his glass, and chinked hers.

"To the quiet life," he said. "And long may it continue."

Then he drained the glass, put it back on the table, and headed to the telephone.

NEXT IN THE SERIES:

LONDON CALLING!

MYDWORTH MYSTERIES

Matthew Costello & Neil Richards

When a prominent family's daughter flees sleepy Sussex to seek a career on the stages of a glittering West End, Harry and Kat are asked to check in on the young woman. But the two of them soon discover that there is a much bigger danger to the woman and her family than mere acting dreams being crushed.

A LITTLE NIGHT MURDER

ABOUT THE AUTHORS

Co-authors Neil Richards (based in the UK) and Matthew Costello (based in the US), have been writing together since the mid-90s, creating innovative television, games and best-selling books. Together, they have worked on major projects for the BBC, PBS, Disney Channel, Sony, ABC, Eidos, and Nintendo to name but a few.

Their transatlantic collaboration led to the globally best-selling mystery series, *Cherringham*, which has also been a top-seller as audiobooks read by Neil Dudgeon.

Mydworth Mysteries is their brand new series, set in 1929 Sussex, England, which takes readers back to a world where solving crimes was more difficult — but also sometimes a lot more fun.

Made in the USA
Middletown, DE
14 April 2020